I0818117

THOUSAND WORD THRILLS

SHORT STORY COLLECTION

RACHEL GRAHAM HAYLEY BERNARD-RYAN

AMANDA JOSEPHINE TANYA KOLB M. A. SAVINO

AND

THIRTY-TWO THRILLER AUTHORS

GRAYSCALE

INK.

This contest and publication is part of the *Author: Unlocked* initiative, dedicated to helping aspiring authors take the leap into writing and self-publishing.

Learn more at author-unlocked.rachgrahamreads.com

ISBN 978-1-067011-58-1 (ebook)
ISBN 978-1-067011-57-4 (paperback)
ISBN 978-1-067011-59-8 (hardcover)

Cover design and interior formatting by Rachel Graham.

Cover image adapted from Zanyar Ibrahim.

INTRODUCTION

One thousand words. One week.

Forty-five writers from across the globe accepted the challenge: craft a gripping short thriller story in just seven days. Each author chose one listed item, and built their story around one of three contexts: *Dating Disasters*, *Neighborhood Nightmares*, or *Spooky Season*.

The energy was contagious. Stories went live for public voting, where readers discovered fresh voices and shocking twists. The top ten earned their way to the finalist round, where a panel of authors, bloggers, and avid readers celebrated the best of the best.

Competition was fierce, with Hayley Bernard-Ryan taking out the top spot with *Last House*, where fairytales turn to nightmares; Amanda Josephine followed in second with *The*

H.O.A., showing what can happen in a neighborhood pushed to breaking point. And third equal: Tanya Kolb's *The Maze*, a tribute to a lost love; and M. A. Savino's *Edward*, where a suspected haunting goes horribly wrong (do they ever go right?).

But here's what made this challenge extraordinary: for many of these writers, this was their *first* experience putting words to page, wrestling with self-edits, bracing for feedback, and preparing their work for publication. They stepped outside their comfort zones, took the leap, and now their words live on bookshelves and e-readers around the world.

If you like the thirty-seven stories shared in this collection, be sure to let the authors know. You could be that motivation they need for their next publication.

Fair warning: you'll find yourself muttering "just one more story," and before you know it, you'll have devoured them all.

Turn the page, and let the thrills begin!

CONTENTS

LELA

BRANDY AKER

Context: Spooky Season | **Item:** Photograph

The sky was cloudy as we turned down the neighborhood of Silverton. The street was empty but, Halloween decorations lined the lawns. Once the car was parked, we all started unloading the boxes into the house. About an hour later, the boxes were stacked in the rooms. We all gathered around eating pizza from the box while talking about what to do next. I headed to my room after eating and went through several boxes. As the sun went down I changed into pajamas and climbed into bed.

The next morning I sluggishly got ready for school. I'd rather my first day not be on a Friday but I have to go. Once I make it to school I glanced at my schedule to see what direction to go. A tap on my shoulder startles me I look up to see a girl "Hi I'm Ava. You're Amelia right?" She asks I mutter a "yeah" before we start down the hall. Thankfully she leads me to my first class before leaving me with a fundraiser form. Once the bell rings, I go into class to start the day. The rest of the day passed by quickly, and now I'm walking home.

After dropping my stuff at home I set out on the sidewalk to fundraise. I hit a couple of houses with no luck where I'm late to the start. There's one last stop on my journey the house in the middle of the block. The house has older decorations which is a nice change. I take a deep breath and slowly head up the walkway. I knock on the door and give a smile when it opens.

"Hello I'm Amelia. I'm fundraising for school raffling a themed basket. Would you like any tickets?" I ask politely and smile. He returns the smile as I hand him the form to look over. After a few moments he hands it back. "I'll think about it. Come back next week sometime. I'm Harold also." He tells me and I nod an say thank you before leaving the house.

On Monday, after school I head over to Harold's house to hopefully make a sale. The house looks silent but I knock anyway and after a few minutes it opens. Standing in the doorway was an older woman and not Harold. She gives me a friendly smile and leans on the doorframe.

"Hi Mrs., I'm here to see Harold about a fundraiser." I say and she nods. I hold the form and she looks at me thoughtfully. "He's not home dear. I'm Lela." She tells me with a hand on the door. I glance at my form then to Lela. "When Harold gets home can you let him know Amelia stopped by please?" I ask and she nods her head slowly at me. "I'll let him know Amelia. It was nice to meet you." She tells me and I nod and say thank you before turning to leave. When I get to the side-walk I wave as she shuts the door before I head home. Lela seems like a nice lady.

Today is Halloween, the day ghouls and goblins roam. I took my sister trick-or-treating and she got a bag full. "One last stop." I tell her before detouring down Harold and Lela's sidewalk. Since meeting Lela I have been visiting to talk to her after school. We talk about a little of everything and just sit on the porch enjoying the decorations. In such a short time we've become close.

I knock on the door and patiently wait for Lela to answer. After a few minutes the door never opens and no sound comes from inside. Looking through the window it looks like no one's been home in days. That's odd that Lela's not home, She's always home. I lead my sister home with her candy wondering if Lela's okay.

The next morning I head over to their house to check on her. I lightly knock on the door and a second later Harold opens the door. He gives me a look like he already knows why I'm at the door.

"I just wanted to come and check on Lela. I stopped by yesterday and no one was home." I explain to him. He gestures for me to come inside as he goes to retrieve a photo-graph. "Here, look at this" he says while handing it to me. "Is this Lela?" he adds as I glance at the photograph. Looking at the picture I see Lela and a little boy in front of the house, but she's younger in it.

I raise my head with confusion on my face. "It is, but younger. Is she okay?" I ask while handing the photo back to him. He gives a frown back before clearing his throat.

"Lela's my mother. She passed a couple years back the week of Halloween. She went peacefully but, she always comes home for Halloween week. I go out of town every year as it's too hard on me being here. She loved Halloween." He tells me with tears in his eyes. I try to wrap my head around what I was just told. "Lela's a ghost but, I saw and talked to her. I feel a little crazy." I admit to Harold as I shake my head.

"I'm sorry you found out this way Amelia. I know she probably enjoyed your company. If you ever need to talk about it don't hesitate to visit. It's okay to feel the way you do about it." He tells me with a small smile and I slowly nod. "I'll come visit and you still owe me for a fundraiser in the future." I tell him with a laugh and he joins in laughter with a nod. I say goodbye and head out the door to the sidewalk. I glance back to see Lela in the window. She smiles and waves at me and I return the wave before heading down the sidewalk feeling at peace.

Goodbye Lela till next Halloween.

ABOUT THE AUTHOR

BRANDY AKER

Hi, I'm Brandy the author behind "Lela"! I am an avid reader and animal lover. I have always written stories since I was younger, but this is my first step into the publishing world (hopefully not my last). Thank you for reading my short story and hopefully many more stories to come.

LAST HOUSE

HAYLEY BERNARD-RYAN

FIRST PLACE WINNER

Context: Spooky Season | **Item:** Photograph

Natalie Tillman would rather be doing literally anything else besides walking her brother through the neighborhood trick-or-treating. She'd disguised herself to the best of her ability--hood up, Covid-blocking mask on (although no one seemed to be wearing them anymore)-- anything to avoid being recognized by her peers. She was fifteen years old, for Christ's sake. She ought to be at a party.

My parents suck so bad right now, she thought.

She glared down at her little brother, who was dressed up as a monster. She found the need to take her anger out on someone. “Your costume looks stupid,” she decided to say.

“*You* look stupid,” Hudson returned without missing a beat.

Natalie raised her eyebrow at him. “This is your last year doing this shit, you know. You’re ten years old.”

“Fineee,” he whined. Then he brightened up, seeing a tall, dark house on the corner. “One more house?”

“Fine,” said Natalie with an epic eye roll. She tried not to smile as she watched Hudson run up to the door. After all, it *was* a big moment for him.

His last house.

The next thing she knew, she was laying on a cold, dirt floor. Wherever she was, it was pitch dark.

“Natalie?” said a small, frightened voice somewhere near her.

“Hudson, is that you? What happened?”

“I... I don’t know,” he stammered. “I rang the doorbell then I was here.”

Natalie sat up slowly, her whole body aching. She reached her hand into her pocket and pulled out her cell phone. She turned on the flashlight and shone it around the room. Hudson was shaking on the dirt floor with his knees drawn up to his chest.

They appeared to be in a confined space that was a little bigger than a walk-in closet. It was a circular room with slimy-looking stone walls. She shined the beam upwards and could not see a ceiling. It was as though they had fallen into a very deep well.

"Can you call Mom and Dad?"

Natalie looked at her phone. "There's no service," she said numbly. She rose to her feet, trying to rein in her terror and be in control for her little brother's sake. Slowly, she walked around the circular space, surveying the strange-looking walls for a way out.

Hudson's lower lip quivered. "Should we… should we yell for help?"

"No," whispered Natalie, the hair rising on the back of her neck as the temperature around her plummeted. She suddenly had the distinct feeling that something was very, very wrong with the room. "No, I think we need to be as quiet as possible…"

Hudson frowned. He opened his mouth to protest, but then he froze.

The walls were growling.

A loud pounding on the door startled Ciaran Donn right out of his reading session. "Go gabh suas leat féin," he muttered angrily to himself. He set the book on the end table beside him and walked stiffly to the door. He held his hand to his aching lower back, feeling every inch his age. To the outsider's eye, he appeared to be a young man in his mid to late thirties, but he was older.

Far, far older.

"What?" he demanded crankily, throwing open his front door to glower at the couple standing in the rain.

The husband had his arm around his wife, who was shaking violently. If the husband was not there to support her, Ciaran wondered if the wife would simply collapse to the ground. The thought made him smile, just a little. People falling over was hilarious.

Especially when they died.

"Our... our children," the frantic woman said, holding up a photograph of a teenager with shoulder-length black hair and a small boy with green eyes. "Please. Have you seen them?"

"Nae, miss," Ciaran said, his dark eyes sympathetic. "Canna say that I have. I'm sorry."

The mother lowered her head, quietly sobbing. The father seemed suspicious, glancing over Ciaran's shoulder and into his house. "One of the neighbors saw them come by this way. Your house is last on this street. Are you sure you haven't seen them?"

Ciaran's eyes darkened. "You don't have any children."

The father blinked slowly, a dumb look spreading across his face. Trembling, the mother watched the children vanish from the photograph until it became a blank paper in her hands.

"We... we don't?" she asked. "Are you sure?"

"Aye," Ciaran said gently as he slowly shut the door. "Good night."

Once he was sure that the Tillmans had left his property, Ciaran Donn walked across the dark room and plopped into his recliner. He leaned his head back and closed his eyes, focusing his attention on the Tillman's house. He sent all the belongings and photographs of the Tillman children into the Place of Doesn't Belong. When the parents returned to their home, all memory that they ever had children would be erased.

Natalie and Hudson Tillman belonged to *him* now.

Ciaran smiled and lifted the book to open it to where he'd left off. He watched the pair of children huddle together in the room. He felt a little bad for them, the room was so dark and plain. He'd decorate it later. At least he'd created the monster to keep them company.

He realized he wasn't in the mood to read a horror story tonight anyway.

He set the book back into the bookcase and chose another.

Fantasy, perfect.

He'd captured the princess when she came to his house dressed as Rapunzel three Halloweens ago.

Sensing she was being watched, the girl lifted her tear-streaked face to stare out of the illustrated page. When she spoke, her whispery voice sounded like the rustling of paper.

"Please. Please, let me out."

Ciaran groaned. So ungrateful. With the power of his

mind, he created a land of magical castles, gorgeous landscapes and carriages-- just for her. What else could a little girl want?

His face spread into a slow smile.

Dragons...

ABOUT THE AUTHOR

HAYLEY BERNARD-RYAN

Hayley Bernard-Ryan is a dark fiction writer who lives right outside Philadelphia. She is the author of the horror fantasy novel "Wrathburn" and the young adult horror novella "The Hookman Legacy". Several of her short stories have appeared in various anthologies such as "Thrills and Chills: A Halloween Anthology", "Table for Ten: A Horror Anthology" and "Xmas Thrillers: Frostbite". When she's not frightening readers with her writing, Hayley enjoys drawing, traveling, going to concerts, running and watching old movies.

FLESH AND MUSCLE

ALAINA BLACK

Context: Dating Disasters | **Item:** Mirror

I trotted over to the front door as I heard it open. Anthony had finally come home from work.

"Hello, dear," I smiled, pecking him on the cheek as he put down his coat.

"Hey," He muttered, getting out his phone and walking past me to the living room.

I followed him, finding him already seated on the couch. He hadn't looked at me once. I stood in the doorway of the room for a moment, not exactly knowing what to say or do. I hesitated before sitting next to him on the couch.

"How was work?" I asked, trying to get him to acknowledge my existence.

"Fine."

"Are you hungry? I made dinner."

"I'll eat later," He still hadn't looked up from his phone.

"Your mother called me earlier," I mentioned it casually, though even the thought of my mother-in-law annoyed me, "She's coming over in a little while."

"Uh-huh."

"She called me irresponsible and said someone like me shouldn't have married someone who's actually important," He finally looked at me.

"What do you want *me* to do about it?" Anthony's words were harsh, "*Honestly,* Mae, you're such a child. You can't accept it, but you know she's right."

I watched him as he stood up and stormed off, likely to our bedroom, where he would lay in our bed and do nothing productive. Like usual. I stood up and went to the bathroom. Looking in the mirror, I saw tears in my eyes. That normally happened when he acted like this. His words always hurt.

I wiped my eyes and took a moment to collect myself. I knew I shouldn't cry. After all, it was almost every day that he acted like this. I *should've* been used to it, but I wasn't.

Slowly, I walked to the kitchen. I wanted to give him one more chance. Opening the microwave, I grabbed the plate of food I'd already made for him and dug through the drawers for a fork and knife. After collecting the food and silverware—along with a few napkins—I made my way to our bedroom.

I gently knocked on the door, not waiting for a response before opening it. Anthony barely spared me a glance before continuing to scroll on his phone.

"I know you said you weren't hungry, but I figured you might want to eat something eventually," I spoke softly, hoping he wasn't still upset with me.

"I don't want your food," His voice still held the venom from before.

"I know, I just thought I'd—"

"*I. Don't. Want. It*," Anthony's voice held an undertone of warning, one that I was very familiar with, "The food you make has always been disgusting, anyway."

I stared down at him, the anger that I felt threatening to spill over. I hated him so much. All those years of horrible insults and bruises hidden by makeup suddenly came back to me. I grabbed the steak knife off the plate.

Moving quickly, I lunged at Anthony, allowing the plate of food to clatter to the floor. He hardly had the chance to react before I stabbed the knife into his throat and swiftly dug it across the width of his neck. Blood spurted from the gash in pulses, painting our once-off-white sheets a deep red. It was *so beautiful.*

I stared at what I had done for a while. Anthony was still conscious, for now, and was making a pathetic gurgling noise. I glanced down at the blood-soaked knife in my hand before stepping away from his upper body. Looking down at his legs, I came to a decision and began tearing through the top of his pant-leg. Once I had removed the fabric, I began slicing into

Anthony's thigh, cutting a medium-sized chunk out of it. The gurgling had stopped.

I took the chunk of meat and began slowly walking back to the kitchen, leaving a trail of crimson in my wake. Once in the kitchen, I grabbed a baking pan and gently placed the meat inside. It was still oozing blood. I seasoned the chunk and put it in the oven.

I knew I didn't have time to clean up Anthony's body before my mother-in-law came over, so instead I cleaned up the path of blood I'd made to the best of my abilities and washed myself up. After changing my newly stained clothes, I made a couple of sides to go with dinner.

About thirty minutes later, I served a plate of food and placed it neatly on the table with some silverware. As I did this, there was a swift knock at the door. I quickly walked over and opened it to find my mother-in-law's already disappointed face staring back at me.

"Mildred, hello, I'm so glad you were able to come!" I said, fixing a pleasant smile on my face.

"Uh-huh," she pushed past me and walked into the dining room, "Where's Anthony?"

"There was a problem at his work, so he'll be staying late tonight," I said, following her and taking the seat across from where I had set the plate.

As Mildred sat down in her seat, her expression turned to one of disgust.

"What *is* that?" She said, staring at the meat.

"Pork," I explained simply, still smiling.

“It looks horrible,”

I didn’t respond. Instead, I waited for her to pick up her silverware and cut a small piece of the meat off. She did, stabbing it with her fork and lifting it to her mouth. Blood was still in the meat, though it had turned brown and gelatinous from being cooked. She hesitated before placing the small bite into her mouth. It seemed to physically pain her to keep chewing, but she did, swallowing with an exaggerated gulp.

“It’s disgusting,” Mildred’s face held revulsion, with a hint of fear. Fear that what I had fed her wasn’t pork.

“I know it is,” I smiled even wider, appreciating the fact that I had just watched my mother-in-law eat her own son.

ABOUT THE AUTHOR

ALAINA BLACK

Hi! My name's Alaina and I'm a but new to writing. I've never actually had a book published, although I have gotten another story published through a competition like this one. I love anything horror related and my dream is to become a successful author and publish loads of books for people to enjoy!! :]

NEIGHBORHOOD WATCH

CARLY BLACK

Context: Neighborhood Nightmares | **Item:** Photograph

Every evening since I moved in, Brian sat on his front porch. Watching. A gargoyle, but his cathedral was the cul-de-sac and his stone ledge a lawn chair. Whenever my car turned into the driveway, he'd wave. "Neighborhood Watch. Keeping us safe."

I forced a smile, grabbed my groceries, and quickly locked the door. Through a gap in the blinds, I watched him watching.

That night, a note appeared on my doormat: *Be careful. I see everything.*

Morning brought another wave. "Long day at the office?"

My throat tightened. I had never told him where I worked. A notebook sat open on his lap, pen tapping the margin as if documenting my answer. Last week I caught him jotting down my friend's license plate number.

Amber light glowed on Keeley's porch two houses down. The door swung open with a laugh, cartoons humming inside. She pulled me in and pressed a wine glass into my trembling hands.

"Did he write that?" Keeley's eyes were wide.

I nodded, unfolding the note.

Keeley snorted. "Classic Brian. He's harmless. He's just obsessed with his watchdog routine. Unsettling though. I had a guy follow me home from work once. Filmed me through my windows for weeks before I caught him. Terrifying. But Brian? He's just lonely and weird."

"It feels like he's cataloging my entire life. When I leave and come home. When I took the trash out at midnight once, he was there."

Keeley's son piped up from the carpet without looking up from his crayons. "Mom says we don't like Brian." The drawing beneath his small hands showed a figure with a square head and impossibly elongated arms that stretched to the paper's edge.

Keeley leaned closer, voice dropping. "So, *we* keep an eye on him instead. If he steps out of line, we'll know."

I laughed, half-convinced. Wine kept pouring. Cartoons kept humming. For a little while, the world felt secure again.

Brian called a neighborhood meeting Thursday. Billie Jean

complained about missing mail. Tom mentioned his doorbell camera caught someone prowling at 2 AM.

"Where's that guy from the end house?" Billie Jean asked.

Keeley crossed her arms. "Marcus? Total loner. Gives me the creeps."

Others murmured agreement. Marcus never waved back. Kept odd hours. Had those dark curtains.

The next few days shredded my nerves. Someone rifled through my trash. I woke to faint rhythmic scratching at the back door.

A second note appeared under my windshield wiper: *Don't go out alone at night.*

When I showed her the note, Keeley's mouth tightened. "You're staying here tonight. I mean it. Grab your things." Keeley pulled me into a hug.

"Should I contact the police?"

"Without actual proof? It could be Marcus, Brian, or someone else. Predators like that don't stop until someone forces them to. We're swapping spare keys just in case."

When Keeley left, I called the non-emergency line. My voice shook through the explanation: the notes, the constant surveillance. The dispatcher sighed and promised to "make a note of it," then hung up mid-sentence. That hollow click made everything worse.

I stared at the phone. No one was coming. No one believed me.

That evening, I discovered muddy footprints leading straight to my bedroom window. The latch hung open an inch. I always locked it. My palm pressed against the cold glass, breath fogged the surface. Someone had attempted to get inside.

Sleep wouldn't come. I lay rigid in bed, staring at nothing, until a thin beam of light sliced across my curtains. My breath caught in my throat.

Brian stood on his porch, sweeping his flashlight across driveways and hedges. The beam lingered on my bedroom window, slow and deliberate, before drifting on. Taking inventory in the dark.

He claimed to keep the neighborhood safe. But perhaps he was the danger.

On Thursday night, a bang rattled my front door. Frozen, I clutched the phone tight.

Brian's voice cracked through the dark. "Rachel! It's not me. Keeley…"

It didn't register. What about Keeley? Keeley would help. I couldn't breathe. I dialed, fingers shaking.

Keeley's voice crackled through. "I'm on my way. Stay inside."

Brian pounded and shouted warnings I couldn't understand. Then headlights swept the driveway. Keeley's SUV. Relief flooded through me.

Keeley ran up, something metallic caught the light. Brian spun toward her. "Rachel, you're in danger! It's not me."

The blade flashed. Brian's hand flew to his neck, blood poured between his fingers.

I screamed. Keeley grabbed my shoulders, steadying me.

"It's over." Voice calm. Controlled. "You're safe now."

Police arrived. The story assembled too easily: Brian, the creepy neighbor known for harassment, finally snapped. According to Keeley, he had a knife and lunged at her. Protective and brave, she fought back.

One officer shook his head. "I'm not surprised it ended this way with a guy like that."

Another clapped Keeley's shoulder. "We'll need to bring you both in for questioning but seems like clear cut self-defense."

I nodded along numbly unable to shake the uncertainty.

By dawn, Brian's body was gone, and the driveway was scrubbed clean. Keeley walked me home, promising to check in tomorrow. "You don't have to worry anymore." I wanted to believe her.

That evening, I wandered through my too-quiet house. Every window locked. Every light blazing. Something was off.

My favorite scarf, the one I thought was lost at the laundromat, lay draped over a kitchen chair. A grocery receipt from last week, thrown away, sat folded on the counter.

The phone buzzed. Text from Keeley: *Wine tonight? You need company.*

My gaze drifted to the window. Keeley's amber porch light burned steadily across the way.

Then I saw it. A photograph tucked under a fridge magnet, one I hadn't placed there. It showed me asleep in bed, taken from inside my room. My phone sat on the nightstand, its screen showing a timestamp from after Brian died.

Beneath it, another magnet held a child's drawing in crayon. Stick figures with X's for eyes. Red smears clutched in crude hands, a woman's hands.

Pulse hammering. Brian's last words crashed back: It's not me.

Keeley waved through the window. Her smile was bright, warm, and wrong.

The air left my lungs.

He'd been trying to warn me all along, and she had my key.

ABOUT THE AUTHOR

CARLY BLACK

Carly Black writes twisted tales for readers who like their thrills laced with shadows.

Whether she's unraveling a chilling mystery, exploring the dark corners of the human mind, or crafting a slow-burning psychological suspense, Carly brings emotional depth, layered tension, and unforgettable characters to every page. Her stories blend gripping plots with atmospheric settings and just enough dread to keep readers up past midnight.

When she's not writing, Carly can be found buried in true crime documentaries or hunting down the next indie author to read. She believes the best stories are the ones that linger long after you've turned the last page.

carlybwrites.com

THE MAN

CEDRICK "DRIPPY" BOUCHER

Context: Spooky Season | **Item:** Photograph

There's a mystery man who breaks into your house during the midnight hours, he walks through my neighborhood every night to see which idiotic human even dares to test out his little game. This game is where you have to do a ritual to allow his overwhelming power to infuse into your house, speak in his native language, and blast the air conditioner with frigid temperatures to make your home vulnerable to him. I started doing the right thing so I could make the ritual perfect, I spoke the language of his name and I set my thermostat to 30 degrees, now the only thing is to wait, I waited and waited, I started getting bored and finished designing my dress for my sister.

Wedding next week, about an hour passed, and no one was breaking into my house. I just laughed in my head, I knew this sick ritual was a scam and really tried to do it, I pushed off the couch to the thermostat to put the heat on but as I walked to it....it was gone? "The hell?" I said, looking around to see where it had gone, Am I losing my mind? As if anything couldn't get any weirder, my door flew open and a strong gust of wind blew through, I was sent flying through my kitchen, my head hitting my cabinet so hard that blood shot out of my nose. I tried to catch the blood from getting everywhere but it was too much. "DAMNIT!" I shout out, I stand up from the kitchen to run to the door to close it but the door was missing, just like the thermostat; the door was gone. "What is going on?!" I started to panic, the blood was increasing by the second I had to do something quick, this man was really.......I took this game as a joke but now I believe it. I run upstairs to my bedroom to see if there's a way to stop this BS, I booted up my laptop to the fan site of this "game", half of the posts of people explaining some of their loved ones got kidnapped, others are romanticizing the mystery man, but one post stated something I needed the most.

How to stop the "Mystery Man ritual"

08 October 2002

If you are reading this, you have probably allowed the

> demonic spirit of "The Mystery Man" into your own house , I found one specific way to get the spirit out of your house. Step one, find the man, try to locate him in your house, find signs of a moving object and faint noises of moaning. Step two, have any camera, a Polaroid, a digital camera or even the camera on your phone is okay. The third and final step, find this man and take a picture.

The post ends, I read over this post over and over, just thinking it's a stupid idea. But it's the only thing that could work, I pulled my drawer and pulled out my digital camera. I came out of my room and walked sneakily down the stairs trying to see if nothing catastrophic would happen, I looked around my house for any signs of where he could be but it was silent, the only thing that made noise was the cold blasting air and the groaning escaping my body as my bloody nose got worse. But I started hearing the faint noises of moaning coming from the mud room, I staggered my body to the room to see a disturbing sight that unfolded in my mind. Blood splattered all across the room, the blood was unknown but it was making my entire body ache, and my stomach wanted to throw up. "What-WHAT THE ACTUAL FUC-" as if a literal censor bar covered my mouth, the room started converting into a painting from France, my head was spinning and I freaked out to the point I just took a picture of the room, as doing so the room stopped. I looked around in the distorted room, all the mangled walls and decor binding into my brain like a tattoo, I looked at the photograph I took of the room and my heart sank lower than ever before, there was a man, a extremely tall man that was consumed with darkness that you can even see yourself through, his eyes were filled with malice, and a smile that look like it came from a cartoon character, looking at the image made my spine tingle. I stood up from the room and looked at the door and immediately stopped, the man was standing in front of me, his smile widened by the minute as his slender long hands began to reach me, he opened his mouth and the language of voids escaped. "Vel thûr'ash na'hrel vorthen." His voice low pitched, something that could come right out of a professional bass singer, my brain started racing but quickly stopped and was turned to sleepiness, I looked up trying to stay awake so I don't pass out....but it was too late, my mind was starting to shut down, the last thing I saw was him reaching to me....after that, it was just darkness...

Unknown time later.....my eyes widened, I started vomiting out blood and chunks of meat. "I doubled over, 'Hrrrk—BLLLUUURRGHH!' then snapped upright with a piercing 'Aaaaaaaghhh!'" I started hyperventilating and crying, I shuffled away from the place I vomited and bumped my head on an iron box, my back felt the cold metal and jolt. "Ah! What the heck." I noticed that I was stripped of my clothes only leaving me in my undergarments. "Shit! My clothes, where the hell are my clothes?!" I started looking around my area, getting a grip of where I am. “Where am I? This isn’t my house.” I looked in the corner and saw a bucket with some newspaper, a chained ball that they put around prisoners’ ankles, “this isn’t my house anymore...I gotta get out..now.”

TBC..

ABOUT THE AUTHOR

CEDRICK "DRIPPY" BOUCHER

I'm a incoming young author who just wants to make people happy..

THE OLD ABANDONED MANOR

TAYLAH BOX

Context: Spooky Season | **Item:** Broken Phone

On a cold Halloween winter's night, four teenagers had come across an old eerily abandoned manor as they were walking down a street with other houses around them that were also abandoned, and had no lights on so it was like a ghost town. So the teenagers had decided to come back later after the Halloween party and after they dropped their siblings back home, when they later escaped after arguing about going to a Halloween party with the whole school being there, their parents were yelling at them "NO" because they were too young, so later in the evening when their parents had gone to bed, they all had snuck out to go this party and had a great time till it was starting to get past midnight and nearly everyone went home, but when there were some friends left they decided to play a game, Truth or Dare?

Mia was the daredevil, a rebellious child which made a big influence on Jaxson, Sarah and Joel, these four teenagers had all grown up together in a small town called Moe where everyone knew everyone and you could not get away with anything because words and rumours can spread very quickly. As everyone had left this party a few kids decided to stay behind with Mia, Jaxson, Sarah and Joel. Everyone had come to an agreement about playing truth or dare, friend 2 had asked Sarah truth or dare, in which Sarah replied with "Dare". So friend 2 had dared Sarah to go to the old abandoned manor and stay there the night, but Sarah was scared and didn't want to do this alone so Sarah had asked her best friends if they wanted to do it with her, in of course their response was "Yes".

As the evening went on, Sarah, Joel, Jaxson and Mia grabbed flashlights, some food, sleeping bags and all the essentials they would need to be able to last the night, but what they didn't know was that some spirits come out to play when it is Halloween and everyone is welcome.

The manor had big old wooden doors, with door handles and hinges that were once gold and are now brown, due to the rustic and old feeling with paint fading off the wooden doors. When the four teenagers had arrived, the doors had opened by themselves and everyone started to get scared, deciding whether they should continue with this dare or not but a dare is a dare and you must go through with it otherwise something horrible will happen to you.

So as they went into the manor the doors had slammed shut by themselves and everyone had screamed while Mia had thought she had seen someone in the corner of her eye, she had described this shadow figure to the group but no one believed her.

So without knowing exactly who she is, Mia had secretly explored the manor by herself while the others were clearing some space downstairs and setting everything up. Mia looked in the study room where she had found some old notes and an old diary but as she started to read some things had started to happen like all of a sudden Mia had suddenly felt a bit chilly but there was no windows opened and things started to fly across the room, as she had gone further into the manor Mia had found an old pamper room with an old mirror that was dusty so she tried her best to clean the mirror. As she was cleaning the mirror she had seen the lady again but her eyes were not normal, the lady's eyes were red like the devil.

As these things started to happen Mia had run back to the group screaming, "A Dare is A Dare if we do not go through with this then one of us will die." Mia had told everyone to keep saying this and keep it going through their heads in case they had gotten scared. But as the night went on things had taken a turn for the worse, the ghosts kept moving things around the house, prank calling through an old broken phone, and little white orbs kept appearing in old photographs.

There was no electricity running through the manor so the teens searched the manor for a candle as, they even looked in their backpacks and as they thought no one could find any Jaxson had come prepared he had yelled out "I found a candle in my backpack" but then Sarah had also found a candle in an old demolished kitchen and she had brought them in to what looked like a loungeroom from what was left.

As the night went on Mia had started to show the rest of the group what she had found when she went exploring, more and more things kept happening so they decided to do a seance to help release these angry trapped ghosts because they were angry that people were in their home, their safe haven but they wanted to escape and leave their home to move on. When the sunrise hit of the morning on the next day, the manor was quiet, not even an eerily feeling as the group had a look around and realised that Sarah had made it through the night and through the dare, as she looked at her friends they all had made it with her, they are stronger together but get weak when they are not around each other.

The morning after, the day had become brighter, the sun was shining and everyone was happy.

ABOUT THE AUTHOR

TAYLAH BOX

Just a girl who loves coffee and books Love reading all kinds of genres especially dark romance smutty books Australian Born

Join the Bookish Beauties Facebook group

IT'S ALL BLUE NOW, BABY.

M. A. BROOKES

Context: Dating Disasters | **Item:** Mirror

Enrico's is 'our place'. At least, that's what he says.

He picked it, of course, but then he always picks the places. He likes soft lighting and hushed tones, says they discourage me from '*making a scene*'. He also likes Italian food, and, more tellingly, he knows that I *don't*. He knew that before our first date too, all those years ago, but he still brought me here. Another red flag I happily ignored.

He sits across from me now, older. His face a grey, restless mass flickering in the candlelight. He looks tired. But then, he *always* looks tired now. '*Tired of your shit*' he likes to say, ever the charmer.

A small smile curls the stubbled corners of his thin lips. He hasn't even bothered to shave. It doesn't really matter, though, not when the smile is as hollow as the eyes that seem to look straight through me as he raises his glass.

"To us." he says.

My hands remain firmly in my lap. I don't even raise my glass. He doesn't seem to notice. He never does any more.

He orders for me, as always. The salmon. Always the salmon. The waitress comes and goes quickly. She must sense the atmosphere. She smiles at him. A small, sad, *sympathetic* smile and a slight tilt of her head. Pity and professionalism in equal measures. If only she knew.

I look at his hands, clasped together in front of him on the table. They're looking old. Cracked and calloused. '*Worn to the bone, providing for you, not that I ever get any gratitude...*'.

He still wears his ring. He's never taken it off. Even after everything. That must mean something, right? The thought conjures guilt, and I reach my hands out to touch his. He pulls them back without even looking at me, and all I grasp is cool, empty air. A cold void where his warmth should be. It's no surprise. I can't remember the last time we touched. It's been a year since we've had any real connection. A year to the day since he completely shut me out.

The drive home is silent. We pass the old cinema, its neon lights flashing over the rain-slicked street, but we don't stop. Not like we used to. A meal and a movie soon became just a meal. We barely even have that now. My salmon sits in a crinkled doggy bag in the back seat, the steam of its residual warmth slowly creeping up the rear window. These days, I just don't have the appetite.

We pass the park where he proposed. The old oak we sat under now just a dark skeleton against the twilight sky. He doesn't look, just grips the steering wheel harder as he speeds past, his knuckles white against the dark leather.

He's humming our song, the one we shared our first dance to. I wonder if he even knows. It's hard to tell. Sometimes, it's like he doesn't even see me, like he's trapped in his own world, one I'm no longer a part of. I'm just a passenger, tethered to his side by a promise we've both failed to keep.

He pulls onto the driveway and kills the engine. I wait for the words, the vitriol, the anger, for the real argument to start, just like last year.

But it doesn't come.

He just gets out of the car and walks up the path alone. He no longer opens doors for me.

Inside, the house is cold. It's always cold. In the living room, our wedding photograph still stands on the side, a fine layer of dust sitting like a halo around the frame. I drift towards it to wipe it away, pulled by an invisible thread, but I don't. I can't. What's the point?

I follow the well-worn path up the stairs. The bathroom is how we left it. His razor on the side, untouched, my perfume bottles collecting more dust. I turn to the mirror and look for myself in the broken glass. There's nothing there. There hasn't been for a long time. Just an empty space where a woman used to be.

A low hum pulls me from the room, back down the stairs. A familiar sound. I know where he's going, he's heading for the garage, and I know what that means; it's time for me to go to bed.

He flicks on the single bulb, which fizzes in the silence. The garage is neat. He likes to keep his space neat. All his tools hang from the walls in perfect formation, the floor scrubbed clean. I smell the faint scent of bleach still hanging in the air as I follow him inside. He's carrying my bag of left-overs as he heads for the large chest freezer in the corner. He runs his hand over its smooth, cold lid, before he opens it with a soft click, a cloud of icy vapour spilling up into the air. I see his breath fogging as he leans over and looks down.

And there I am.

My hair is feathered with frost, each strand a delicate silver spiderweb. My skin is a pale marble of whites and blues that match my dress. He always liked that dress. He always said blue was my colour. Well, I guess it's all blue now, *baby*.

Leaning in carefully, he places the bag into an empty space by my shoulder. A tear slips down his cheek and lands on mine. He gently runs the back of his fingers across my frost-bitten face to wipe it away. He's always so gentle now. Far more gentle than he was the last time he laid his hands on me. But it's too late. The tear has iced into a tiny, perfect diamond. A fitting gift for our special day.

"Happy anniversary, my love," he whispers as he places a tender kiss on my frozen brow. "Until next year."

He closes the lid and leans his forehead against the cold metal, his body shaking with quiet sobs.

I watch from the doorway.

Silent and unseen.

Just the way he likes me.

ABOUT THE AUTHOR

M. A. BROOKES

Multi-genre Psychological/Speculative Thriller Author.
Debut novel: 'The Girl With The Blue Tick' Coming soon.

THE SALEM SLAYER

MARIE CASHEL

Context: Spooky Season | **Item:** Candle

As I pass the sign with a witch on a broom welcoming me to Salem I look over at the book resting on the passenger seat. The cover is designed to look like a 90s VHS and staring back at me is the same sign I just passed that now says 'The Salem Slayer" with blood dripping down the sign.

My mind wanders to the memory of receiving the book in the mail anonymously. I started reading it that night and quickly became determined to solve the biggest cold case of Salem history.

The next morning I was planning my trip to Salem for Halloween.

I pull up to the BnB I will be staying at and see that it is completely decked out for Halloween. I am removing my bags from the trunk when an older lady exits the BnB and greets me.

"Welcome to Time Weaver BnB! I am Emily, you are going to have a magical time!"

"Hi! I am Kaitlin! I am so excited to be here for Halloween!"

I stop halfway up the steps when I realize that a now pale Emily is staring at me. I follow her eyes and see she isn't staring at me but is staring at the book in the nook of my arm.

Emily looks up at me and says "Where did you get that book?"

Confused, I say "Um... I got it in the mail a few months ago. Not sure who sent it to me though. I want to solve the case! Were you living here when it happened?"

Emily sighs, "Sadly yes, It was only a few years into me running this BnB! On Halloween in 1994 a masked psycho went on a violent rampage around town. After killing seven people they disappeared never to be seen again."

Emily's eyes glaze over as if she is reliving the events of the past.

"More people had flocked to Salem for Halloween that year because Hocus Pocus had come out a few months before. The whole town was buzzing with excitement but the killings blew out that excitement faster than you can blow out a candle! Most people think the killer was a Halloween fan who came into Salem to kill people and then moved on to kill elsewhere but I think that the suspect is a local who still lives in Salem."

Processing everything Emily has shared and ready to continue my investigation I rush up to my room. I am exhausted from my long drive but ignore it as I spread my notes out on the bed and flop down on my stomach to continue my research.

I wake suddenly and realize that I fell asleep mid investigation. It is dark in my room but when I flip the switch to turn on the lamp it doesn't work. Using the light of my phone I walk over to the room's main light switch and flip it to the up position bracing my eyes for the light...nothing happens. I flip the switch a few more times but when the room stays dark I realize that something is wrong.

With my phone battery being at 15% I decide to go find Emily to see if she has any flashlights. I am stepping out of my room and jump in shock when Emily comes around the corner with a light that looks like a candelabra. As she gets closer I see that it is not an electric light but an actual flame candle. Before I can further process the fact that she is using a candle she sees me and smiles at me. In the low light and flickering flame her smile is distorted and creepy.

"Dear we had a power outage! This happens sometimes right around Halloween! Here is a candle that will light up your whole room!"

"Do you have any flashlights? Then I won't have to worry about it blowing out"

“Oh no I don’t have any working flashlights unfortunately but this candle will be just perfect for you!”

“Umm ok... do you know when the power is expected to be back on? I need to charge my phone and laptop.”

Emily’s smile suddenly looks more ominous, or maybe it is just what she says next that unsettles me.

“Oh don’t you worry about that! It is late and tomorrow is Halloween! You will be so preoccupied that you won’t be thinking about your phone! Here take this candle...”

She puts the wick of the candle into one of the flames of the candelabra. The flame spits a bit and gets brighter before transferring a flame to the candle.

I stare in awe at the newly lit flame as it emits a purple hue.

“How does it have a purple flame??

She gave me a small smile and said “A local witch who made it infused it with cream of tartar which causes the fire to turn purple and increase energy fields. I must insist that you use this candle tonight while the power is out.”

“Uh ok...thanks” I say as I take the purple flame candle from her and step back into my room.

Hoping that the power will be restored in the middle of the night I plug my now dead phone and blow out the purple flame.

I wake up thinking about the weird interaction with Emily and the candle with the purple flame. I roll over and see the now extinguished candle on the bedside table sitting next to my still dead phone.

Halfway down the staircase I freeze when I notice that the wallpaper and decor looks different. Did Emily stay up all night to make it feel like we went back to the 90s?

Walking around town I admire what look like vintage 90s Halloween decorations that have been put up.

A flyer in a shop window catches my eye and I feel suddenly woozy. This has to be a joke right?

BIG HOCUS POCUS PARTY TOMORROW OCTOBER 31, 1994.

To Be Continued...

ABOUT THE AUTHOR

MARIE CASHEL

Marie Cashel is a proud childless cat lady who works as a director of human resources at a law firm in Washington DC.

When she isn't working she enjoys spending time with friends, reading, and cuddling with her orange tabby cat, Peter Pan.

Marie has always loved reading and after being encouraged by family and friends she has finally started writing her own stories. The Empty Library is her first published story!

instagram.com/bookscoffeeandcats13

LIKE YOU HAVE A CHOICE

DAVID CRYPT

Context: Dating Disasters | **Item:** Broken Phone

I tug at the hem of this damn dress again, my fingers trembling more than I want to admit. The bar hums around me, but I can barely hear it over the pounding in my chest. I'm almost done with my espresso martini. Sam should be here by now, and with each tick of the clock, a creeping unease coils in my stomach.

I tell myself this time it better work. I'm not sure if this little black dress will even fit me again. I'm close to hitting the big 4-0. Do I really have it in me to keep spending nights hoping to find my prince charming?

My thumb hovers over the screen for what feels like the

tenth time. No message. My pulse quickens. Each flicker of the bar's neon lights makes me flinch. At this point, I almost hope he cancels so I can go home...or maybe even talk to Mr. Rugged Smile across the room. I don't mind a dad bod and scruffy beard, but if he's too scared to come talk to me, would I really want him?

A tap on my shoulder yanks me from my thoughts. I turn to meet those gorgeous blue eyes attached to a golden-haired man with sharp cheekbones I know well.

"Heyyy, I'm so sorry! Promise this isn't like me," Sam says with an apologetic smile.

"No worries, as long as you get the next round," I say.

Sam and I matched through SoulSpark, an exclusive app that guarantees your soulmate on the first date. No wonder it costs an arm and a leg, but at this point, I am desperate.

We talk for hours about family, dreams, and ambitions until the bartender yells, "Last call!"

Outside, he holds my hand as we walk, and I hold his. With an affectionate smile, I think, maybe SoulSpark got it right. *On the first match? Impressive!*

At my car, we hug. Longer than normal. He doesn't say goodbye. Instead, his arms clamp around me, unyielding. My chest presses tight, breath shallow. I look up and see his normally charming eyes darken. They are now hungry, sharp, almost feral. Panic claws at me as I struggle, but his grip doesn't loosen.

My stomach twists. Panic claws at me as my hands struggle to push him back.

"Get off me!" I snap, finally shoving him back.

"Come on, baby, why don't you just come home with me?" he says with a mischievous smirk.

"Fuck off. I'm not going anywhere with you especially if you're going to act like a creep!"

I pull my keys from my purse and get inside my car.

He watches me as I drive away before he walks back towards his car. I flip him the bird, and I'm off to my house, cold sweat on my forehead.

What the hell was that! Soulmate on a first date, my ass!

I enter my house, swing off my shoes, and then I get a ding on my phone. I check and see it's a notification from the dating app. Fingers shaking, I read:

Congratulations! You've advanced to Round Two!
Date confirmed Friday 10/31/25.

Round Two? I haven't agreed to anything. Dread pools in my stomach. "I'm definitely not going on a second date with that predator", I mutter.

I call Ryan, my best friend who's also using the app.

He answers after the second ring. "Hey Gwen, back from your date so soon?"

I tell him everything about Sam and the "date".

"Anyways, I'm calling because I got a confirmation for a second date. Did anything weird like that happen to you?"

"No, I'm barely going on my date with Mark next week. So excited!"

We say our goodbyes after he proves no help.

At a last attempt for information, I scroll through a Reddit forum about SoulSpark. One post makes my fingers freeze: a woman had received the same message...then vanished after her date. Apparently her family still can't find her. Comments whisper about being "chosen" for something.

The word echoes in my mind: Chosen. Chosen for what?

The next few days blur in paranoia. Friday evening, every creak and gust of wind makes my head snap toward the door.

At 8:00 p.m. sharp, my phone buzzes. Then a loud *Ding!* ricochets through the house. I fumble my phone, dropping it hard on the floor. A jagged crack spreads across the screen, slicing through the words that make my breath catch in my throat:

Your Perfect Match has arrived!

Three loud knocks follow. My heart races. It can't be.

I decide to get this shit over with and let Sam know who he's messing with.

I swing the door open. Sam stands there, smug smile cutting through the dark porch light. The night air feels colder, heavier.

"Time to go, pretty lady," he says, stepping forward. Then he freezes.

He walks straight into the barrel of my Glock pressed to his chest. Sam's smirk falters, but only for a moment. "You won't do shh....."

BANG!

A loud clunk explodes through the night. Sam collapses onto the porch. My hands shake violently, gun slick with sweat. Heart hammering, I barely register the red-and-blue lights as Ryan steps forward, bloody flashlight in hand.

"Good thing he didn't hear me coming," Ryan says, breathless. "I just wanted to come check on you and saw you were about to blast this guy so I figured I'd help. I called the cops as soon as I saw this man lurking around your house."

Minutes later, the cops cuff Sam, medics check his head, and we tell our story. Self-defense, plain and simple. I pick up my shattered phone. The cracked glass reflects my pale face and those chilling words one last time.

"Let's delete the app, it's supposed to be used for finding people...but not the way we thought" Ryan says firmly.

"Yeah," I whisper. "I'm done with this mess."

ABOUT THE AUTHOR

DAVID CRYPT

Hi, I'm David! An avid psychological thriller reader who finally decided to write one myself. This short story is my first attempt at stepping into an author's shoes, and I'm glad I did. It gave me a realistic taste of what writing might be like.

As a reader, I've often thought "I wish the ending was stronger", or "Was that the twist?" So, I took this chance to create the kind of story I always wanted to read.

The feedback from readers has been incredible, and I'm grateful to everyone who took the time to support and critique my work. The thriller community is nothing but welcoming, and maybe this is just the beginning for me.

Keep and eye out for more under my pen name: David Crypt.

facebook.com/DavidCryptAuthor

DEATH DIARY

TANDY CYRUS

Context: Dating Disasters | **Item:** Diary

Bryn crept silently through the hollow house. Her footsteps softened by the high-end carpet beneath her feet. His penchant for high class items would help be his undoing, well that and the gun she was carrying. She knew where he would be. In his home office with a glass of scotch, some ridiculous news show on his television excessively working and not giving a damn about anyone or anything else.

She felt like she knew him even though they had only been dating a few weeks and in some ways she did. She knew his type, and they pissed her off more every day. Entitled, good looking, smug, condescending, and gaslighting assholes. The world would be better off with one less in it.

Closer now she could hear him on the phone.

"Well Gil that's why I pay you. You need to clean this mess up. Yes, I am well aware how I look in the media being caught with another woman right after Amy's death but that's what I pay you for. Fix this. She's an old friend consoling me. Spin this."

This guy is unbelievable, she thought. She also wasn't the girl that he had been pictured with but that didn't matter to her anyway. This wasn't about that. Amy hasn't even been gone 3 months, and this jackass had moved on. Oh, sure Amy had her doubts as she often poured out in her diary but mostly, she wrote about the abuse versus the infidelity. Bryn had been repulsed by his attitude the first time she met him in person at the bar but kept a warm fake smile on her face while she tried to ward off the nausea that he was causing.

She had stalked his habits for weeks before she "accidentally" bumped into him. She was professional like that. Not one strand of hair out of place in her bun, glasses that perfectly framed her heart shaped face and a smile that put anyone at ease. Is it wrong that she should be trying to help him versus killing him? Sure, but who cares about ethics? It sure in hell was not this guy.

Bryn entered the room, but he didn't stand a chance against her and her Glock 9 with the silencer. Brett spun around at the sound of her and his eyes went wide with shock at the sight of the gun.

"You!" He exclaimed before hitting the ground.

Bryn heard a voice holler from downstairs.

"Brett!! I'm here! Are you upstairs?" Bryn didn't count on this since the owner of the voice attended Pilates on Wednesday evenings and should not be here. It was Lucy the bimbo from the picture that he was so worried about.

Luckily for Bryn she knew the massive house had two sets of stairs with the second one leading to a back door. Bryn took one last look over her shoulder and hastily maneuvered the stairs and was outside. Adrenaline took her through the wooded area at the rear of their property and onto the adjacent street where she had parked the vehicle she used. Bryn hit the gas and was on her way before the first scream rang out.

Lucy was surprised to see the front door slightly ajar but didn't think much about it as she called up the stairs to Brett. She went to the kitchen to get a drink. She was supposed to be at Pilates but decided to come to him instead. Things were looking up for her since she started dating him a few weeks ago. Well, a few weeks according to the press that she tipped off to see them. She of course had been in his bed the better part of two years waiting on that wife of his to die.

She headed up the stairs and stopped short at the door. Brett was laying on the ground with a dark red spot spreading out across the front of his tailored dress shirt.

Lucy ran to his side. She checked his pulse and pulled out her cellphone to call 911.

"911 what is your emergency?"

"Help me my boyfriend has been shot." Brett opened his eyes and looked at Lucy. She leaned further down to try to make out what he was saying.

"Dr.... Dr...."

"Shh, I know you need a doctor. Stay with me Brett."

In that moment he shut his eyes and drew his last breath.

Six months later....

"Lucy Wingate?"

"Yes, that's me," answered Lucy.

"Doctor Evans is ready to see you now, follow me."

Lucy took a shaky step forward. How fortunate she was to get an advertisement in the mail about this doctor. One of the best trauma and grief therapists in the state. Lucy had only dated Brett according to the world for a few weeks, but his death had hit her to the core since they had been having an affair for two years. She needed to process and move forward.

She was so sick with grief and anger that the police couldn't find a killer. His security system had been shut off due to him anticipating her showing up. She had told him a million times to just give her the code, but he had refused while Amy was alive and now, she felt responsible for his death.

Lucy took a deep breath and followed the receptionist through the door. She felt immediate relief at seeing the doctor. There was not one strand of hair out of place in her bun, glasses that perfectly framed her heart shaped face and a smile that put Lucy at ease. She had a soft voice when she spoke.

"Hi Lucy. I'm glad you are here. My name is Dr. Evans. Dr. Bryn Evans and I'm here to help you. You can help me get to know you a little better by writing in this diary I'm going to give you to bring back to sessions. Have a seat and we will get started."

ABOUT THE AUTHOR

TANDY CYRUS

Tandy Cyrus lives in Ohio with her husband, Jared, and three children. She's also a mom to a plethora of animals including two dogs, a pot belly pig and a small army of chickens and cats. She works as a mental health therapist and enjoys hanging out with her family, baking, reading and interacting with the psychological thriller community in her spare time.

WELCOME TO DAGHANTOWN

ERICA DAMON

FINALIST

Context: Neighborhood Nightmares | **Item:** Note

Sara had just started her new job at the Daghantown city office. The position wasn't glamorous, but it paid the bills and didn't ask questions. As long as she showed up, smiled at people, and didn't ask about the locked door in the break-room, things were fine.

If you don't ask, they won't either.

Then she met Maria, who'd worked in the records room for about eight months. She asked all the questions.

"Where'd you work before?"

"Will you stay here long?"

"Want kids?"

"A dog?"

Sara brushed them off and tried to move on. This was her fresh start.

Four months later, Maria didn't show up for work. First one day, then two. Then a week. But the oddest part—the part that raised goosebumps on Sara's arms—was that no one asked where she was. No questions. No concerns.

That same week, Sara heard a thump behind the locked door.

Later, she caught Shawn, the city clerk. "I heard something in that storage closet."

"That's not your concern." His words were taut.

She stepped toward the closet. "But I swear..."

"Get back to work. Being nosy will only get you in trouble." He stared until she returned to her office.

Sara started taking her lunch breaks in the records hall, poking through the dusty files.

Over the last decade, eighteen women had worked there for exactly a year before they abruptly stopped showing up. One could be ignored, or even two or three leaving without giving notice, but *eighteen*?

It took a few weeks to build up the courage to ask about it. She marched up to Shawn's office, blustering past his assistant, and banged on the door.

"Yes?" His annoyed voice echoed across the room.

"Where's Maria? And Rebecca, and Melanie? All the others? Do you know how many people go missing from here?" She was too worked up to stop the accusation in her voice. At some point, she'd decided Shawn was somehow behind this. Should she have gone to the cops? Maybe, but that wasn't an option for her.

He stood up, fingertips going white as he leaned over his desk. "We don't ask those kinds of questions here. If you'll remember, we didn't ask about your past. We didn't ask about theirs either. It attracts a certain type; it's not my fault they are flighty, barely staying long enough to become locals. Employees move on. That's how things are."

Sara stepped back. The things she hadn't wanted to talk about—was it possible those women had similar stories? Could she imagine leaving like that too?

"Thank you for coming to me with your concerns. Please see yourself out." He gestured to the door, and she slunk away.

She was halfway to the stairs when a sound stopped her. It was the assistant, his wide eyes beckoning her. When she stepped up to the desk, he slipped her a folded piece of paper, shaking his head slightly as she went to open it. "At home," he whispered.

At home, she pulled the note from her purse.

> THEY DIDN'T QUIT. LOOK UP DAGHANTOWN DEMON.

The first internet search didn't turn anything up. Which felt strange. She tried a few other queries and finally got a hit. It was some sketchy paranormal blog, but it mentioned the town and the city office. And missing women.

> The Daghantown Demon resides at City Hall. Not much is known about its true form, but it feeds on women to keep the town fertile. Farmland that was once dust turned rich, and local businesses thrived despite the wider economy. Lore further states the sacrifices must be locals.

She lowered her phone. In under two weeks, Sara would celebrate her one-year anniversary.

She reread the paragraph. True form. Meaning... it took

multiple forms? She mentally catalogued everyone at City Hall. Was someone she worked with a monster? No, not someone. Shawn.

It was the day. Her work anniversary. Pulling out her old self was like slipping on the most comfortable pair of shoes. A few extra touches and she was ready.

Ready when Shawn pulled her into the break room. A celebration. *Unlikely.*

The lights were out like it was a surprise party, but no one clapped, no candles twinkled on a cake. But the far door stood open. A dim glow inside, beckoning

The moment she stepped inside, the door slammed, and she was plunged into darkness. Something grabbed her, but as its claws sank into her shoulder, it recoiled. It didn't expect her. Didn't expect the runes scratched into her body.

In the small space it couldn't get away; she was the pursuer now. Grabbing, clawing, fighting until they fell to the floor, her on top, it shivering beneath her. Bound by her spell, tied to the floor by invisible shackles.

"You should have asked." She spat onto the writhing body. Half Shawn, half something else.

Its screech was unintelligible, but she imagined the question.

"Before I came here, back in my old life—you know they only let me out of the psych ward because I had no other symptoms. I wasn't crazy; they just didn't believe me. They never believe people like me. We've seen things, done things. Monsters like you? You don't scare me. I'm more powerful than them. Than you."

She tugged her necklace from under her blouse and slammed the pentagram onto the monster's face. It sizzled, and the smell of burning flesh filled the closet. As the screeching continued, it became increasingly human, a scream—Shawn's voice—until that faded too.

The body withered, becoming dust on the linoleum. Only then did she stand, tucking the pendant away, swiping her hands over herself, and straightening her skirt. She caught her reflection in the mirror on the door, her eyes black marbles, pitch dripping from them like tears of tar.

A quick wipe, a few blinks, and her rosy cheeks were back, blue eyes blinking innocently. As she stepped out of the closet, she really hoped people wouldn't ask.

ABOUT THE AUTHOR

ERICA DAMON

Erica Damon is a writer, equestrian, and artist living in Western Massachusetts. Her compulsively creative nature has led to a collection of 'what ifs?' and that sense of wonder weaves its way into her fiction. She writes thriller and horror under her name, and equestrian romance under the pen name Isla Ryder. If she's not writing, she's likely out riding horses while ideas swirl in the background.

ericawritesisla.com

RED

CLAUDINE DISCALA

FINALIST

Context: Neighborhood Nightmares | **Item:** Glove

I pull my pinky finger out of the drain. Spaghetti-like strands of tendon dangle, the digit slick in my hand. I stare at it and my stomach lurches into the back of my throat. Now I know what happens when you throw yourself between two fighting dogs. I got bit during the melee, ran inside with my pinky finger hanging on by a thread and shoved my shaking, bloody hands under the water. It detached and it slipped in. The stump under the towel pulses.

Jack, my sweet boxer, was attacked by the Cujo-monster-dog who lives next door. It was another gnarly fight. Poor boy. I swear he understands English. Once, I told him I liked red better than blue—he's brought me his red squeaky mouse every day since.

"I know, boy. Just stay still," I say, as he sits on the kitchen floor, bleeding, panting and watching me with his big brown loyal eyes. He does, of course, stay still. He always does what I ask.

We came out here for peace. I left the city, left a guy who broke bones and promises thinking forty-five minutes from town meant safety. It was idyllic, at first. Rolling green hills, ponds, the smell of pine, birds chirping and foxes hopping through meadows. Jack and I had never seen so many stars. I bought a telescope. But peace lasted exactly two days.

On the third, my neighbor appeared. Old truck belching smoke, he leaned out, eyes narrow, teeth yellow, his gloved hand resting on the window frame. It was too hot for gloves, wasn't it? Maybe they were his "murder gloves".

"Hi, little lady. I'm Clay. Man of the property around?"

"That'd be Jack here," I said, instantly regretting it.

Clay looked me up and down, his eyes lingering where they shouldn't. I wished I had lied and said "the man" was at the store.

"We don't like city people in these parts."

How does he know I'm from the city?

Jack leaned against my leg, growling. Clay's Cujo-dog snarled, a map of scars across his hide. The kind that don't come from accidents.

"Shut the fuck up, Tank!" he yelled, smacking the side of the truck, making the dog cower. Clay turned to me. "Mind yourself and we won't have no troubles between us." A cloud of dust choked me as he sped toward his farmhouse.

That night the humid air was filled with howls, screams, men cheering. It made my skin crawl, the fur on Jack's back tense. I aimed my telescope at his yard and learned why Tank had those scars. Dogs ripping each other apart for money. What kind of sick fucks do this? The sounds haven't stopped since.

And Tank hasn't stopped coming. Every time Jack steps outside, Tank ambushes. Gnashing teeth, fur flying, blood soaking dirt. Police tell me to get proof. Meanwhile, my boy collects new scars.

Tonight, I snap. I just wanted a new start. To be left alone. But now my finger is gone, my kitchen's full of blood and Jack's trembling from his wounds. We're quite a pair, alone, abused and trapped inside this house. His sad little eyes rip my heart open. I refuse to live this way again. I grab the phone with my good hand, lay it on the counter and dial my neighbor.

"Listen, asshole—"

"Careful with that tone, little lady." Clay cuts me off, voice raspy through the speaker. "You shouldn't have called the police. Out here, we settle things the old way. Before I do to you what Tank did to your mutt, you and I are gonna have a little fun. You look like a gal who enjoys a good time."

Jesus, no. "I have video of your dog fights. It's a federal offense. Truce or I go to the FBI." My good hand finds the drawer and grips my Magnum. Loaded and ready.

He laughs slow, amused, so clear and close even the hairs on the back of my neck stand and want to run. His next words stop me dead. "Lot of good that will do you when they're forty minutes away and I'm two." The line goes dead.

Fuck!

Fear ignites through me like tiny wires. I've been here before. A man's threats. A house that feels like a cage. My heart races.

Before I move, Jack does. He explodes off the floor, into the screen door, forcing it open, slamming it into the side of the house as he leaps through.

"Jack!" I scream, chasing to the doorway. Too late. He's gone, tearing toward the farmhouse.

He heard the threat.

He understood.

The screaming starts within minutes. Human, high, ragged. Jack's growls are guttural and merciless. Then a silence that could choke the life out of me.

I slide down the door frame, gun shaking in my hand, pain pulsing inside my bandaged stump. Thick, sticky night air presses in. I stare into the pitch black, waiting as unrelenting sweat paints lines down the sides of my cheeks. If I unload this gun and don't do enough damage, we'll be having the "fun" Clay spoke of. Every creak on the porch makes me flinch.

A shadow moves. Oh God. My finger squeezes the trigger back a hair and I stop breathing.

Panting. Nails clicking on wood.

"Jack?" My whisper cracks.

Jack steps into the light, calm, chest heaving but steady. Victorious. Something dangles from his mouth.

Not a toy. Not just a glove. A glove with a hand still inside.

"Drop it," I say sweetly.

He lets it fall at my feet, tail wagging, eyes shining with love, as if he's brought me a gift. A blood-soaked red one.

The same way he did in the city. The same way he did the night my boyfriend disappeared.

Except that time, it was a whole arm.

I don't need to look closer. I know what it means. The danger is gone. Again.

Jack made sure of it.

ABOUT THE AUTHOR

CLAUDINE DISCALA

Claudine DiScala's short stories have won multiple awards. She holds a B.A. in Political Science and a Master of Science in Criminal Justice and spent twenty years as a licensed private investigator in New York, several of those years running her own female-owned and operated PI firm. Some of those experiences may have found their way onto the page though she's not saying which. A member of the International Thriller Writers Association and the League of Utah Writers, she leads a weekly critique group and lives in Southern Utah with her husband, two children and two dogs. She is also a small business owner and advocate for suicide prevention. When she's not writing she can be found hiking, camping, swimming, cycling, running, (and occasionally remembering to sleep)—preferably outdoors and far from her inbox.

Visit her at ClaudineDiScala.com and on Facebook, Instagram, X and Tiktok.

DATE NIGHT

ARTHUR EATON

Context: Dating Disasters | **Item:** Photograph

Gretchen wondered how she had gotten herself into this mess. The cold rain and damp night air chilled her to the bone, and all she wanted to do was get through the meal and try to enjoy herself. Bundled in as many layers as possible, she spotted the "restaurant" (if that is what her date wanted to call it). She managed to find the only pebble on the ground and narrowly missed a swan dive toward the pavement as she heard the snap of her heel. Great. Another thing to add to the growing list of problems for the night. Wrapping her arms tightly around herself, she hobbled toward her destination and prayed with all her might that her luck would change soon.

Her day started to go wrong as soon as she started getting ready for the date. She managed to smear her eyeliner. Even the cat, Atticus, hissed and ran away from her, but not before he sunk his claws into her calf. The blood streaked down her leg, and she giggled a bit, thinking about how it looked like a candy cane. After dousing the tiny holes with a mountain of antibacterial ointment, she continued getting ready. The apartment was a shambles, but she had no plans to return later. The housework could wait. She put down a bowl of food for Atticus, grabbed her coat, squeezed her feet into shoes that were obviously made for a more petite woman, and took one last twirl in front of the mirror. She was ready.

Gretchen climbed the cobbled steps up to the entrance of In Cod We Trust. Judging from the exterior, she decided to keep her expectations low. She walked into the dimly lit foyer and was met with a large "Please seat yourself" sign. Perfect. She took a minute to run her fingers through her hair and to ensure none of the ruby red gloss had escaped her flawless lips, glancing at the TV above the bar to skim the local headlines and sports results. The local high school won its football game last night. A local library was asking for donations. One story caught her attention: "Local woman missing." A chill ran up Gretchen's back as the woman's picture filled the screen. She stared into the deep blue eyes of her twin.

After releasing the breath she didn't know she was holding, she broke out of her thoughts and realized she had a date to meet. It must have looked bizarre to see her stop in the middle of the restaurant. As she looked around, she noticed a lone man sitting at a table in a shadowy corner. Gretchen took another deep breath, smoothed her dress, and made her way toward the stranger. As she approached the table, her date scraped back his chair and reached for her hand.

"Hello, you must be Peter." She made a mental note to work on her pickup lines later.

"Yes! You must be Gretchen. Please sit. I've ordered wine and a selection of appetizers before we eat."

Peter took her coat and slid out a chair for her. She stood for a moment to allow the full magnitude of her outfit to sink in. She had stressed all afternoon about her ensemble and was determined to savor his lingering gaze as she slowly descended into the chair. She grabbed the menu from the table and tried to hide her disappointment at the selection. Sadly, she let her eyes fall to the salads and decided on a garden salad without onion. As she put her menu down, she noticed Peter's eyes were still locked on her. There was an intensity that felt like he was devouring her with his eyes. She shifted in her seat and tried to break the tense atmosphere.

"Do you come here often?" she began. Yet again, she scolded herself for not being more prepared for small talk.

"This is the first time for me. I'm new in town, and the name made me chuckle." His bright blue eyes seemed to twinkle as he laughed. "I was glad you agreed to meet up with me. I was beginning to wonder if something had happened."

Gretchen paused while lifting her wine glass as she

attempted to answer his question, but the words were stuck in her throat.

"We order at the bar. If you will give me a minute, I'll go place our order," he said as he casually brushed a cool hand on her arm. His soft touch sent chills up Gretchen's bare flesh.

Gretchen peppered the meal with awkward questions but found herself only half-listening. Her mind kept wandering back to the news story about the missing woman, her doppelgänger.

"Did you see about the news earlier about the missing girl?" she casually threw into the stilted conversation.

"Have they found the body yet?"

Gretchen paused and realized the date needed to end. She reached for her purse and decided to go. Peter flagged down the bartender and asked for the check.

When he opened his brown tattered wallet to pay, a single photograph fell out and drifted down to the table. In front of Gretchen, the missing girl stared back at her. Gretchen gasped, grabbed her coat, and rushed out of the restaurant. Peter snatched the photo and ran after her.

"Who are you tonight?" Gretchen whispered.

"Who do you want me to be?"

"That's not how this works, and you know it."

Months of planning had led to this night. All the careful preparation. All the practice. And he had ruined it by having a trinket. A memento. So stupidly sentimental.

"Look, I know I messed up. When we picked her, I could

not stop thinking about how much she reminded me of you. I had to have something," Peter shot back.

Gretchen muttered, grabbed Peter by the arm, and dragged him down the street. This year's event had been ruined, but next year would be his turn. She had killed the missing woman and stepped into her life, but now this game was over. They had to start planning for next year.

ABOUT THE AUTHOR

ARTHUR EATON

Arthur likes the darker things in life and can often be found with his nose in a book. When he's not in the middle of a disturbing horror book, he can be found putting together Lego sets and listening to cheesy pop music.

THE ORANGE CLEATS

KAY ELEM

Context: Neighborhood Nightmares | **Item:** Shoe

One

Beep.

The smell of antiseptic unsettles me. Everything hurts. Where am I?

Beep.

"Mrs. Miller?"

I force my eyes open. Bright lights erupt like fire through my skull. And then I remember.

Beep.

"The boys—" My throat cracks. I try to sit up. Strong hands press me down.

"One's pretty beat up, but he'll make it."

Beep.

Relief explodes in my chest, flooding my mangled body with euphoria.

Beep.

That's when I catch it. The word that echoes over and over like a never-ending curse.

One.

Two

"Cam! Let's go!" My voice ricochets down the hallway, bouncing off the walls much like my son. "We're going to be late."

Noise follows as my wrecking ball barrels through the house, opening closets and slamming doors.

"Have you seen my cleats?"

Of course. The bright orange monstrosities the team voted on this season. They're hideous, neon, and look like someone dipped them in caution paint. They don't match anything and haven't helped us win a game yet, but the boys love them, so I do too.

"They're by the door," I call back, grabbing my keys. "Now move it. I want coffee."

Cam appears, bag slung over his shoulder, obnoxious cleats on his feet. Wet leaves litter the ground, making the day smell fresh and uncertain. The sun is out now, but I know what the weather is like here. Opening the trunk, I shove Cam's gear inside and double-check for my umbrella. I try to be fast, but I'm never fast enough.

"Cheryl, hey."

Her voice slices through the air and my patience.

Lisa. The needy neighbor from hell. Cigarette dangling from one hand, infant in the other, I know what she wants.

"Headed to the game, I see. Mind if Rodney tags along?" She bounces the baby, her built in excuse. She's not asking. Not really. She learned early on, when it comes to the kids, I can't say no.

I force a smile. "Is he ready? We're leaving now."

"Oh yeah. He'll be right out."

Ten minutes later, Rodney stumbles across the yard. His neon cleats are untied, his jersey is wrinkled, and his hair is in chaos. He's a walking disaster, but with Lisa as a mom, I can't blame him. Today, he's my disaster. I look down at my watch. My disaster who has us behind schedule.

Goodbye, coffee.

For the entire long drive, Rodney plays games on his phone. The sound of sword fights mixes with the traffic and Cam's sighs. My body craves caffeine, and by the time I find a parking spot, my head is ready to explode.

I find a quiet place to sit when the sky lets loose. Rain dives sideways, dancing under my umbrella. The boys slosh through the mud, orange cleats dribbling, slipping, shooting. They're drenched within minutes. Hair dripping and jerseys plastered to their sopping skin.

Rodney misses a save, and the team unravels. Parents groan, stealing glances my way. I want to scream that I'm doing my best, that he's not mine to fix. He's just the neighbor. And yet, when his shoulders sag and he stares at the ground like he's waiting to disappear, the guilt comes anyway. I fold my arms, hating that I'm here, hating that he's mine to watch, but at the same time grateful someone is. Someone has to.

By the time we make it back to the car, the boys are mud-streaked and silent. No complaints, no chatter, just exhaustion and filth smearing against my once clean backseat.

I want to ask Cam about the game to lift his spirits, but Rodney's presence silences us. All I can do is drive and dream. I dream of Lisa caring—of a world where she shows up, so I don't always have to.

Out of nowhere, headlights slice through the rain.

Brakes squeal. Horns scream.

The silence shatters with the glass.

One

Pain takes over as I float in and out of consciousness. I see flashing lights. Hear sirens. But I don't know where I am. People are all around. Some help. Some whisper.

"Crazy lady. Ran the red."

Are they talking about me?

I blink, and my head screams. I see the car—a mangled mess of twisted metal. An accident. The boys? I try to look around, but everything blurs into a sea of lights and madness.

An ambulance door slams. A metallic taste fills my mouth. I can't find the boys. The smell of gasoline turns my stomach as I try to call out. The impact must have thrown me. Are they still in the car? That's when I see it.

A single orange cleat.

It sits alone in the middle of the road. Washed bright once again from the falling rain. It stands almost surreal amid a sea of broken glass, motor oil, and blood. The sight slams into me harder than the crash itself. My lungs seize, but as hard as I try, I can't scream. The cleat stares back at me, beautifully unbroken as everything around me grows dark.

Beep.

"Mrs. Miller."

Beep.

"One."

One. One. One.

In wild abandon, the tears fall. I try to catch my breath, but it's no use. Oxygen escapes me as I choke on the question.

"The other boy?" The doctor's eyes fall.

Beep.

The truth is written in the silence. My world turns upside down as bile rises in my throat. Thoughts too ugly to say aloud fester alongside my wounds.

Beep.

Two cleats.

Laced and ready for the game.

Tapping annoyingly in the back seat.

Mud-soaked, scoring goals.

Beep.

Two cleats.

Mine to protect.

Beep.

Only one remains.

Beep.

My throat closes around the question.

Which one?

The doctor's mouth moves, but it's all static. Whatever name comes next will haunt me forever.

Beep.

"Mrs. Miller, do you understand?"

Beep.

I don't answer.

Knowing won't save me.

Not knowing won't either.

The single cleat burns in my vision.

Obscene.

Perfect.

Alone.

The last bright thing in a world gone black.

Beep.

ABOUT THE AUTHOR

KAY ELEM

Kay writes thrillers that sometimes feel a little too real—the kind that sneak into your thoughts days later. She's drawn to ordinary people whose lives are upended by events straight out of a nightmare, where emotions run high and choices turn deadly. Between chapters, you'll find her with a mug of coffee in one hand, a to-do list in the other, and at least one kid asking what's for dinner. Her stories remind us that danger can live next door, and that love isn't always safe.

Kay writes what keeps her up at night—stories that might just keep you up, too.

kayelemorg.wordpress.com

MIRROR RORRIM

DANIELLE FEAR

Context: Spooky Season | **Item:** Mirror

Halloween night is closing in, and I'm getting ready for the big scare event in town. My friend Eve hadn't stopped pestering me to go until I finally gave in. Truth is, I hate this stuff. The thought of people jumping out of the dark, the screams, the shadows, it already has my nerves unravelling.

I'm sitting at the dressing table, brushing my hair, trying to convince myself it'll be fine, when something flickers in the mirror. Just a flash, a quick movement in the corner of my eye. My stomach knots. Slowly, I turn to look over my shoulder.

Nothing.

The room is still. I let out a laugh, shaking my head. I'm working myself up, imagining things before the night has even begun. But the unease lingers, crawling just beneath my skin, as if the mirror knows something I don't.

Eve arrives, buzzing with excitement, and before I can second-guess myself, we're off to the event. The place is alive with chaos, scare actors stalking the crowd in grotesque costumes, their snarls drawing shrieks of laughter. The smell of fried food hangs heavy in the air, mingling with the sweet spice of cider. A band thrashes out rock music from a stage nearby, drowning the night in noise. It's almost fun, except Eve has her sights set on one thing.

"The house of mirrors," she says, her eyes glinting.

My stomach drops. I try to protest, but she only laughs, looping her arm through mine. "Come on. Hot chocolate after, my treat."

Reluctantly, we go inside. At first, it's harmless. We stumble and giggle at the distorted reflections. Short and squat, stretched into giants, twisted upside down. For a moment, even I find myself laughing.

Then I see it.

A shadow in the glass, tall and slim. Standing just behind me.

I whirl around, heart thundering. Empty space. Just shifting lights and the echo of our laughter.

When I turn back, Eve is watching me, her smile faltering. "You okay Hannah?" she asks, her brow creased.

I force a grin, brushing it off. “Fine,” I lie. But my reflection doesn’t look convinced.

As we push deeper into the maze, the laughter dies on my lips. Every corner feels colder, tighter, and in the mirrors a shape lingers, a tall, black figure, just out of reach. It hovers behind me, and yet when I spin around the corridor is empty.

“Clever,” I murmur to Eve, my voice too high. “These mirrors… they’re trying to make us think we’re being followed.”

Eve shrugs, expression unreadable. She hasn’t glanced behind her once. Not once.

She must be seeing it too. Because illusions can’t single people out… right? They can’t make something appear to only one person… can they?

A sudden tug on my sleeve. “I’m bored,” Eve says, her tone light, almost breezy. “Hot chocolate?”

Before I can answer she’s already leading me out of the maze. My relief is almost dizzying.

The rest of the night unfolds like a strange dream. We stroll between stalls, we roast marshmallows until the sugar burns and crackles, laugh at clowns who aren’t half as scary as they think they are, even dance a little to the pounding guitars of the band onstage.

It isn’t as bad as I imagined. By the time we leave, I almost believe the figure in the mirrors was just that… an illusion. Almost.

Eve drops me off with a cheerful wave, promising we’ll catch up again tomorrow. The normalcy of her voice is almost soothing. Almost. I unlock my front door and step inside. The quiet is immediate and heavy, as if the house has been waiting for me.

Upstairs, I move through the motions of getting ready for bed. My bedroom mirror glints softly in the lamplight as I sit at the dressing table to wipe away my makeup. For a heartbeat, everything feels ordinary.

Then I see it.

The figure. Tall. Black. Still. Standing behind me in the mirror.

My scream rips through the silence as I fall back, chair clattering to the floor. I scramble away, my eyes darting to every corner of the room. Nothing, just empty air. Just me.

I keep searching but find nothing. No shadow, no figure, nothing but my own wild reflection staring back at me. My heart is thudding so hard it aches.

Am I losing my mind? The thought mauls at me, pulling back memories I've tried to bury. My Uncle Otto, his haunted eyes, his trembling hands. The hospital corridors. The muttered warnings about demons. I used to be terrified of him. Now, I'm scared of myself.

Was he sick... or was he right all along? And if he was...

I force myself back to the dressing table. My makeup is smeared; my face still needs washing. Normal tasks. Normal life. If I just... focus.

But as my eyes lift to the mirror again, my breath catches.

It's there.

Not just behind me this time, over me. Its shape is a void,

swallowing the light, its limbs impossibly long. Black claws curl around me from behind, poised, not quite touching but enclosing, ready to draw me in. A mockery of a hug.

A scream tears itself from my throat and I whip around, ready to see it.

Nothing. My chest rises and falls, gasping. I turn back to the mirror.

Its head is right next to mine now, inches away, dagger-like teeth bared in a rictus grin. I can feel the cold of it, like frost on my skin.

And then it moves.

A low, guttural rasp fills the room, vibrating through the glass, through me. It's not quite a growl, nor a whisper, but something in between, something wrong. My ears ring, my vision blurs.

I stumble back, clutching at the air, but the sound swells, pressing in from all sides. My body won't obey me, won't run, won't scream again. The world narrows to the mirror, to that grin, to the claws reaching until...

Darkness.

ABOUT THE AUTHOR

DANIELLE FEAR

Danielle Fear - Author is a South Wales-based self-published author specialising in psychological thrillers. With a passion for storytelling that explores the complexities of the human mind, Danielle has captivated readers with her unique voice and gripping narratives. Her works are known for their suspenseful plots and intricate character development.

daniellefear.com

THE DARKNESS WITHIN THE FOG

S.B. FELDMAN

Context: Spooky Season | **Item:** Broken Phone

I never believed in ghosts. That was until I became one myself. It's not like you see in the movies at all. My life never flashed before my eyes; I never saw a bright white light, and no angelic voices were singing and welcoming me to heaven. I was alive, and then I was dead and a ghost. That's it!

The last thing I remember was walking down the street, coming home from the Halloween bonfire, then a sharp pain in my head. Next, I was walking in a fog on the same street, but I felt so cold. Where did this fog come from? Why am I so cold? It was fall, but it was almost seventy degrees at midnight. I went to check my phone, and the screen was shattered and covered in something dark, warm, and sticky. My phone was not broken before. What is happening? I brushed my dark hair back behind my ear, and that is when I felt it. There was a gaping hole in the back of my head, right behind my ear on the left side. I tried screaming, and nothing came out. That is when it hit me. I am dead, I am a ghost.

I sat down in the middle of the street while the fog and the darkness grew around me. Why was I still here? Wasn't I supposed to like to move on and go to heaven or whatever? I am only 17 years old; I have not done anything particularly good or bad in my life. I looked at my shattered phone again, and it still lit up. The cracked glass showed a message, "call to mom failed." I don't remember trying to call my mom. I got a strange dread racing through me. What if my mom never finds out what happened to me? I don't remember seeing my body. That's why I'm still here, I thought. For closure.

I walked along a street I had walked my entire life, to the only home I had ever known in my brief life. I found out that, unlike in the movies, I could not just walk through a door. I stood outside the front door for what felt like forever. I am guessing only about a couple of hours had passed, my curfew was one, and my mom must have noticed I still wasn't home. I heard the lock in the door click, and then the door opened. My mom walked out onto the porch and sighed. "Where is Jessie?" she said aloud. I tried to grab mom's arm, but I could not. I tried to tell her "I'm right here," but nothing came out. She turned to go back inside, so I followed her.

Mom slumped on the couch and picked up her phone. She

was trying to call me. “Voicemail,” she said, “that’s strange,” she thought aloud. It was strange, I was a teenager and was always on my phone. I watched as my mom slowly drifted off to sleep, gripping her phone in her hand. Mom woke up, startled by something, “Jessie,” she yelled. She looked at the time on her phone and realized it was almost four in the morning. She ran to my bedroom with me right behind her. She pushed through the door and saw my bed, empty. She pulled out her phone and dialed 9-1-1.

The lights were blinding, red and blue shining in every window. Mom explained to the police officers that this was not like me to not come home, I always answered the phone when she called, no, I would not run away. The room grew deathly silent, and then suddenly, a high-pitched ping noise echoed through the house. Mom grabbed her phone off the coffee table and looked at the screen. “New voicemail,” she stated like a question. “I didn’t even hear my phone ring,” she said. Mom looked quizzically at her phone and asked the officer, “Is it ok if I check this?” The officer shook his head yes. Mom held the phone up to her ear and pressed the voicemail icon.

A distressed voice broke through the silence, “Mom!” I heard my voice say through the phone. A scream roared through the speaker on the phone. Mom’s face was as white as a sheet. “That’s Jessie,” she said in a panicked voice. The voicemail call timer continued to tick on. There was no sound for a solid 15 seconds. I am sure that to my mom, it felt like a lifetime had passed. “Mom, he’s right behind me,” I heard my voice say. "Who is behind you, Babygirl?" Mom asked the phone. "It's a man, in a police car, he is going to ……. Mom, he is going to kill me," the voicemail cut off. Mom looked at the officer, who stared back in disbelief. Ding! Mom's phone vibrated. New text message on mom's phone said:

> Mom, Officer Stanley killed me. He hit me on the head with his baton. Look in the trunk of his squad car.

I looked at my shattered phone in my hand. Message sent, the phone read. I had managed to type out and send a text message to my mom. Mom shoved past the police officers congregated in the living room; she ran out to the driveway, "Look in the trunk of Officer Stanley's car!" she screamed. The officer closest to the car popped the trunk, looked in, gasped, and promptly shut it. "Ma'am, you don't want to see her like that," the officer said. Mom crumpled to the ground like a folded paper, her cries piercing the darkness and the fog that had now started lifting. At least she did not have to wonder what happened to me; she could lay me to rest. A gunshot rang out. I watched as Officer Stanley took the coward's way out, and with him, he took the secret as to why he killed me.

ABOUT THE AUTHOR

S.B. FELDMAN

S.B. Feldman is an Iowa-based writer drawn to the quiet darkness that hides within ordinary life. Her fiction lingers in the spaces between fear and fascination, exploring the fragile boundaries of human nature. A lifelong reader turned storyteller, she finds inspiration in the eerie stillness of small towns, the weight of secrets, and the beauty of things left unsaid.

She lives in Iowa with her husband and their loyal dog, Bodhi. She is endlessly inspired by her daughter, stepdaughter, and granddaughter — three generations of strong women who remind her that light and shadow often share the same edge. This is her first published short story.

This story is dedicated to my daughter Kathleena. Thank you for being my rock and best friend for the last 23 years!

POLISHED SOULS

KIRSTEN GALE

Context: Spooky Season | **Item:** Mirror

Emily loved the quiet precision of her job as a dental assistant. The sterile hum, the scent of fluoride, the order—it was a world of control. At 28, she'd worked three years for Dr. Harlan Burr, a silver-haired man whose gentle manner calmed patients. His practice, tucked inside a Victorian building, had creaky floors and lofty ceilings that once charmed her. Lately, they chilled her.

It all started with the dental mirrors. Dr. Burr owned a collection, some antique, passed down from his father—some etched with faint, unidentifiable symbols. Emily sterilized them daily, polishing until they gleamed, their surfaces impossibly smooth, almost liquid in the light. One October afternoon, she lifted one toward the window. In its reflection, her eyes seemed wrong—hollow, shadowed, as though another presence lurked behind them, watching, breathing with her. She blinked. Nothing. Just fatigue, she told herself.

But that night, as she turned the lock and stepped into the silent office, a prickling awareness crawled across her skin. The mirrors along the shelves glinted in the moonlight. Then, one by one, their surfaces darkened, black as tar, swallowing the reflected light, as if a shadow had slid behind each pane. A low, almost imperceptible whisper seemed to drift from the glass, brushing her ear with a cold promise.

Her heart thumped in panic. She wanted to run, yet her legs felt leaden. Finally, she tore herself away, flinging the door shut behind her. Outside, the crisp night air carried relief —but the sensation lingered: eyes on her back, patient, unblinking, waiting.

The next day during Mrs. Abernathy's cleaning, Emily handed Dr. Burr a mirror. In its reflection, something lurked in the widow's throat. It vanished, but her heart raced.

"Everything okay?" Dr. Burr asked.

She nodded. "Fine."

Later, alone, she angled a mirror into her mouth. At first, only tongue and teeth. Then her molars shifted in the reflection, revealing a void where a pale, grinning face peered out. She dropped the tool, shattering the silence. When she picked it up, only her frightened expression remained.

As the days dragged on, the visions worsened. One late afternoon little Tommy Reynolds laid back in the dental chair and when he opened wide the mirror showed not a cavity but tiny wriggling shapes in his gums. Tommy felt nothing, but Emily's hands trembled. A teenager with braces revealed wires that writhed like serpents. Another patient's reflection showed lips sewn shut, though the boy chatted easily with Dr. Burr. Each vision lingered after appointments, gnawing at Emily's mind.

Online research revealed nothing—mirrors were just tools, invented in the 1800s. But these felt alive.

"You've been jumpy," Dr. Burr remarked at lunch. She confessed about the strange reflections.

He chuckled, patting her shoulder. "They're old tools. My father collected them. Halloween's playing tricks." But his eyes betrayed more.

That night, she dreamed of endless hallways lined with mirrors, each one whispering her name. Sometimes she saw Dr. Burr waiting at the end, smiling, holding the ornate mirror like a lantern.

One restless evening, she returned to the office. Moonlight washed the Victorian facade. Inside, she gathered the twelve mirrors and laid them in a circle on the exam room floor. Sitting at its center, she whispered, "Show me."

The surface rippled. A memory appeared: a Victorian woman strapped to a dental chair, mouth forced open as a shadowy figure—Dr. Burr's father? —probed with a mirror. Something slithered from its surface into her throat. Emily gasped, dropping it. Another mirror flashed faces of past patients, their mouths open in silent screams.

A creak from the hall froze her. Dr. Burr stepped in, silhouette stretched by dim light. In his hand was a mirror larger than the rest, its ornate handle etched with strange symbols.

"You know," Emily whispered.

He nodded. "My family's legacy. These aren't tools but vessels, crafted by an occultist in the 1800s. They reflect not light, but souls—capturing echoes of pain. My father fed on those fears. As do I. I was only ten when I first watched him—back in 1898."

Her stomach lurched. "Feed? On what?"

He tilted the ornate mirror. Her reflection stared back, older, hollow-eyed, her mouth a black abyss. "We dentists delve where others fear. The mirrors bind us to it. I thought you were ready, but you've seen too much too soon."

He lunged. Emily grabbed a mirror from the floor. Their reflections collided, energy sparking. Visions poured into her: Dr. Burr as a boy, watching his father drive patients mad, siphoning their vitality to keep himself young.

Desperate, Emily smashed her mirror against his. Shards flew, releasing a chorus of screams. Dr. Burr staggered, his skin wrinkling, eyes sinking—his stolen youth collapsing in seconds, his true age clawing through the facade. In the fragments, she watched him unravel until he collapsed, the ornate mirror slipping from his grasp—then, with a final, hollow gasp, he was sucked into its surface.

Emily picked it up. In its depths, her reflection smiled back—independent, hungry. The mirrors had chosen her now. They whispered promises of power, of youth drawn from the fears of others.

She left the office with the mirrors in her bag. Patients would come, unsuspecting. She'd polish the tools, feel their gaze. Dr. Burr? Officially retired, they'd say. But Emily knew better. He was still there, trapped in the glass, watching. And sometimes she could hear his faint, rasping whisper echoing through the silver surfaces.

As Halloween neared, children roamed the streets, pillowcases heavy with candy, laughing and shouting. Emily's lips curved in a knowing smile. The sugar would bring them in soon—parents already fretting over sticky teeth, chocolate-stained smiles, the inevitable need for a cleaning. She imagined the small bodies climbing into the chairs, eyes wide and trusting, the mirrors reflecting not just their teeth, but the fear she craved.

Emily chuckled. Her hand was steady as ever when she lifted the mirror. Patients leaned back, unaware of the new hunger behind her calm eyes.

"Open wide," she said softly. The cycle had begun again.

ABOUT THE AUTHOR

KIRSTEN GALE

Kirsten Gale writes stories that blur the line between memory and madness. Drawn to the shadows of the human psyche, she crafts psychological thrillers that expose buried secrets and fragile realities. When she's not lost in her next plot twist, she's creating new worlds or exploring the emotions that inspire her work.

Her debut novel, Where Ladybugs Go to Die, is a haunting dive into trauma, survival, and the echoes of what we try to forget. Her follow-up, Never Knock Twice, invites readers to step into a chilling world where curiosity can be deadly.

www.authorkirstengale.com

facebook.com/kgale78
instagram.com/kirsten.gg.78
tiktok.com/@believeinyourself1078
goodreads.com/kirstengale
amazon.com/stores/Kirsten-Gale/author

A COWBOY'S QUEENDOM

ROWAN GLYNN

Context: Dating Disasters | **Item:** Broken Phone

Gazing out the window of her Manhattan office, Kaylie longed for more. Less Actually. The shimmering lights of the city rippled across the Hudson like silk. Queen of high-dollar real estate, she clawed her way up from a cramped apartment in Harlem eating Ramen, to champagne nights. She fought for this life, yet the sirens and concrete jungle felt more like a cage than success.

That night she poured a glass of Cabernet and, on a whim, downloaded Cowboys4Queens. A dating app that promised "Urban queens meet rugged cowboys. Forever sunsets included." Before re-thinking her intentions, she posed for a selfie, bright smile reaching her emerald eyes, face framed with bouncy curls, toasting the camera. "31YO, sassy, BFM, Manhattan Queen seeking simplicity: farmhouse, horses, sunsets on the back porch. Is my cowboy out there waiting for me?" Kaylie hit submit before she could delete it and closed the app.

By morning, her phone had blown up with notifications. Truckers, oil riggers, wanna-be-ranchers. Half-heartedly swiping through them over her morning latte, she was at least entertained. Until that one.

Weather-beaten black Stetson, tan skin, propped against an old fence, surrounded by wide-open spaces. His message read, "My Manhattan Majesty. I'm Romero, 33, Texas-born. Looking for my queen to end the loneliness of my desolate South Texas ranch. Every sunset reminds me of a beauty I've yet to hold. Are you that beauty?"

The flutter of possibility resonated in her chest. Before stopping herself, she responded, "My Tequila Texan, what time should I be ready for our date?"

Within minutes, her phone's notification went off. Romero had replied, "On my way, darlin'."

Feeling a moment of bravado, she typed out her office address. "I don't play games. Don't waste my time or yours if you aren't serious."

That afternoon filled her with disappointment not hearing back from him.

The next day was full of closing paperwork keeping her mind occupied until a knock on her office door. Her assistant's flushed face peeked around the corner, "Kaylie, um, there's a man here to see you. Says you're expecting him."

Her assistant's response was unusual leaving Kaylie to peek through the blinds of her office. Holy shit!

Romero was real. Broad shoulders, pearl-snap shirt, starched Wranglers, and boots worn from work, not fashion. The office hens were clucking all around him.

She inhaled, stood tall, and declared, "Well, if it isn't my Tequila Texan."

Eyes only for her, Romero tipped his hat. "My Manhattan Majesty. You shine brighter than any city lights."

It should have sounded corny, but it didn't.

Dinner was perfect, maybe a little too perfect. He knew her favorites – from food to wine. When Kaylie teased him about it, his answer was evasive, "I just do."

He painted Texas to perfection: bright skies, wide-open spaces, sunsets that made silence seem holy. His gaze lingered, as if she were already his.

"What if I visit?" Shocked by her own response, it was too late to change it.

That familiar smirk was back. "Why wait?"

Knowing it was impulsive, she agreed, "One weekend."

Friday brought Romero to her office, flowers in hand. The hens swooned; one even whispered, "I'd snag that one if I were you."

Back at her apartment, they ordered pizza and toasted with tequila. She found him charming and confident. Easy enough to relax around as the warmth of the tequila flowed through her veins. Midway through packing her suitcase, the floor started to tilt.

"Tequil…stron…" Unable to complete her thoughts, darkness swallowed her.

Catching her, Romero eased her to the floor. "City life poisons the body," he murmured. "Rest, my queen. I've got you."

Eyes heavy, sunlight slipped through wooden shutters. Unfamiliar bed, smell of fresh-cut grass…panic seized her.

Slowly creaking open, Kaylie jerked toward the door. Leaning against the frame, hat in hand, smiling as if this was the normal start to their everyday, stood Romero.

"Welcome home, Manhattan Majesty."

Her voice quaked with fear, "What have you done, Romero?"

Taking a slow step toward her, he replied calmly, "Only what you asked for, a simpler way of life."

"No! I agreed to a visit," she yelled. "This is kidnapping!"

Blurred memories registered slowly. Pizza. Tequila. His Voice. Darkness. "You drugged me."

Tension appearing in his stance, he replied, "I simply eased your fear. You city girls don't know how to relax."

Voices echoed from below. Female voices. Kaylie shoved past him, stumbling down the creaky stairs, then froze.

At the table sat five women – different ages and races.

Silence enveloped the room. Their eyes downcast avoiding her gaze. One nursed an infant; another caressed her swollen belly. Silence pressed heavier than any words could.

Kaylie unleashed her anger, “Who are you?”

The young woman nursing met Kaylie’s glare with tired eyes. “Hello to you too. I’m Sadie, woke up here two years ago with promises of a simpler life.”

Nodding at Kaylie, another spoke up, “Maria. Arrived six months ago.”

One by one, the same story unfolded: promises, arrivals, entrapments.

Nausea overcame her. Kaylie shook her head violently. “No, I won’t….”

Romero’s suffocating presence filled the room. “See? Friends. A family waiting to grow.”

Looking down, she realized Romero had kicked her cell phone across the room after crushing it with the heel of his boot. “There will be no calls,” he said pointedly.

Avoiding her questioning stare, the women’s shoulders sagged under invisible chains. Sadie glanced up. “No escape. Cameras everywhere. Electric fences. Towns too far to run. No neighbors.”

Anger ignited in her soul, “I won’t live in your nightmare.”

Romero’s gaze locked onto hers. “You call it a nightmare now, but you will soon feel at home.”

Blazing with colors she once longed for, sunsets no longer felt like freedom. They now bled across the landscape like a warning.

Unsure if these women would become allies or enemies, Kaylie knew one thing: queens weren't chosen, they were born.

Romero thought he had chosen his queen.

Kaylie would reclaim her crown.

ABOUT THE AUTHOR

ROWAN GLYNN

Most will know me as Karen, aka The Tx Lit Chic. I chose a pen name for the contest as I wanted true, unbiased, objective views of my work. Being the first ever, completed work, I'm satisfied with it. I do hope to bring Kaylie to life in an expanded version of this story as it's been requested by several wanting to know what has gone through my head to finish it off. I am working on a few more stories as we speak, but my ADHD keeps me struggling to stay on track. Some day there may be more from me, until then - my reviews, blog, and social media will continue to feature Indie authors. I hope you enjoy the start of Kaylie's journey.

www.thetxlitchic.com

RED VELVET

RACHEL GRAHAM

Context: Dating Disasters | **Item:** Shoe

He slams me against the wall, pressing his body against mine, pinning me there. The acrid taste and smell of beer oozes from his throat, permeating my nose and making my taste-buds shrivel.

"You give me my treat, then we'll go get you some birthday cake, hey birthday girl?" He breathes into my mouth. "What's your favourite?"

He shoves his tongue in, not waiting for an answer. I almost choke on it.

Red velvet, I think. *But this might just spoil my appetite for it.*

I glance past his face to look around the room. His apartment is small. Dim. There's probably a smell to it, though I can't tell over the rot that is his breath right now.

This was meant to be my birthday treat to myself, but this guy… maybe this wasn't my finest choice.

And now we're alone, in his apartment. If he overpowers me, will anyone hear me scream?

I have to keep him calm. Not give him a reason to get upset.

I push at him gently, testing if he'll ease up.

He does. He smiles a drunken sneer, then takes my hand and drags me toward the couch. He stands me there, then collapses onto the couch, legs spread and hands behind his head.

"Dance for me, birthday girl."

My face deceives me—my mouth drops open and brow narrows.

Dance…? This mother-fu…

But I have to keep him calm.

I smile awkwardly at the so-called "man" in front of me. He leans back on the couch, biting at his lower lip, trying to replicate every bad porno he's seen in some attempt to… what? Seem cool? Get the girl?

But, we're alone in his apartment. No one else knows I'm here.

I do as I'm told.

Keep him calm.

I sway slowly on the spot, moving my arms like a slow

motion jellyfish in the most awkward and unsexy seductive dance that has ever been attempted.

He beckons me over, and I oblige, moving as gracefully as I can towards him, still sprawled on the couch.

Keep him happy.

He reaches out and grasps my hips. I stiffen at his touch.

"What's wrong, birthday girl? Don't be shy." His hands are too tight on my hips, I couldn't twist away if I tried. His tug pulls me off balance, and I fall onto his lap. I scramble awkwardly against his grip, trying to find my balance again, trying to get traction to maintain command over my own body.

Keep your cool.

But he's stronger than I am. He holds me there, despite my resistance. Despite my obvious reluctance to be wedged so awkwardly like this against his thigh.

"There's my girl," he coos.

It'll be over soon...

This dating and mating culture is the weirdest, most dehumanising experience. Match online, chat, meet, fuck, ghost.

Yet, just like everyone else, here I am partaking. My birthday treat.

... then you can disappear like you were never here.

"Mmm, Sasha," he pulls me ever-closer and purrs against my neck. I roll my eyes. That is not my name.

You were *never here, not the real you...*

My hands grab out to stabilise myself, one landing on the couch, the other on his neck.

... for exactly this reason.

His pulse beats under my palm, his skin as smooth as velvet.

Can't have nights like these following you home.

His pulse is strong, regular... and getting faster.

He's getting excited, but I need him calm. I consider pulling back, but I remain frozen in place. I need him calm, not mad.

Keep him calm.

"Shhh," I hush gently, whispering it into his ear.

Keep him happy.

I reach back toward my shoe.

Keep your cool.

"Why are you shushing me, babe?" he says against my neck.

It'll be over soon.

"I need you calm."

Shit, did I say that out loud?

He laughs at this, and sits back to look at me. "Need me calm? Calm's no fun. Why do you want me calm, birthday girl?"

You'll disappear like you were never here.

I smile sweetly at his question, his eyes filled with youthful, randy eagerness, before I whisper: "Panic spoils the meat."

His eyebrows knit together in confusion. Then his lip curls up, and another small laugh escapes him, a second before I slice through his carotid.

The tiny, concealed knife cuts through his skin like butter.

His eyes widen, but it's over before the panic sets in and toughens the meat.

You were never here, not the real you.

For exactly this reason.

Can't have nights like this following you home.

Blood pours out over his velvet skin as I peel a slice.

Red velvet.

My birthday treat.

My favourite.

ABOUT THE AUTHOR

RACHEL GRAHAM

Rachel Graham is a mental health nurse and author living in New Zealand with her husband, two dogs and cat. Rachel's writing is informed by her work, where she's learned that the most interesting characters are those still figuring out their own stories. The publication of her debut novel *Follow Me*, released in June 2024, legitimised pyjamas as her workplace attire.

Follow her (no pun intended) across all social media @rachgrahamreads or visit:

rachgrahamreads.com

facebook.com/rachgrahamreads
tiktok.com/@rachgrahamreads
goodreads.com/rachgrahamreads
amazon.com/author/rachgrahamreads

THE TBR KILLER

KRISTI GUTHRIE

Context: Neighbourhood Nightmares | **Item:** Diary

The room is plunged into darkness as Krislena turns in shock, tripping over her diary and dropping the book she was currently reading by the lamp. The thunderstorm outside rattles her body as the lightning hits not far away and she's plunged into darkness and frantically looks around her. It's silent except for the thunder, bold and brutal as if sounding off cannons.

She feels her blood pressure and anxiety spike up. "Hello?" she calls out. Nothing but the rain meets her question. She tries to stand up quickly in the darkness as her idea of a cozy night reading is quickly forgotten. “Hello?” She calls out again but this time firmer and agitated.

She hears a chuckle in the hallway and turns, fear and terror, a mask upon her face now, her green eyes wide in shock. The adrenaline in her body surges through her veins as she looks in the darkness for anything to grab and use but there is nothing as she cries out “Who are you, what are you doing in my home, I swear to God you best show your face to me asshole!”

Suddenly the lights cut back on as she realized it was the electricity and Georgia Power with the weather so bad she had a black out. Now with the lights back on her eyes seek the hallway. She gasps as a tall, distinguished man of about 6’1 lanky and smiling, nods his head at her.

“Who the fuck are you?” She moves closer to the door as the tall man moves to the door as well. “I would not do that if I were you. In fact, pick up the book you dropped.” “What the hell?” She cries out. He stands even taller and proceeds to repeat himself. “I said, Pick up that book!”,

His tone is more demanding now. She backs away, stepping back to retrieve the book, hearing the tone in his voice and her body trembles. “If you will just pick up the book and put it back on the table that would be nice and proper of you Krislena.” “But how do you know my name?” She bends down and retrieves the book, fingers trembling as tears begin to seep out of her eyes.

Grasping the book she lies it back on the table and faces him, tears and mascara running down her cheeks.

"You may or may not remember me but I wish you had remembered me better. Had that happened I would not be here now. You see, I am an author. In fact I am an author you spoke with many times yet I do not look familiar to you? That is devastating indeed." He moves a step towards her. "I had such great hopes for you and for myself. Do you not know who I am?"

She looks closer at his clothes, his eyes, and shivers with the intensity of his dark gaze of silver eyes, as a tinge of darkness gathers there as if in anger. "I honestly…I'm trying." She fumbles for words as he lashes out "Just stop, you're making it worse!"

He whispers "I'm going to approach you and you are not to MOVE at all. I will then explain who I am Krislena. I repeat if you move this will be even worse for you."

Krislena feels the horror as she stands still clenching her fists as he moves in front of her. "I am Jonathan Sills. I am the writer that you told me my Book, "Shudder in the dark", would be read and reviewed by you, 3 MONTHS AGO!" He screams as her bladder releases and she pees, a pool of urine at her feet, but she remains stoically still.

"I am so sorry, I do remember and I am going to read it." "YES YOU WILL and you will do it. "YOU WILL START MY BOOK NOW!" Spittle flies from his mouth as he thrusts the book he has been carrying into her hands.

"Shall we start? Sit down where you were. DO IT!" She frantically holds the book and sits where she was sitting before and opens the page. He stands behind her as he grabs the rope out of his pocket. "Start reading it to me Krislena. Show enthusiasm for my book as you do the fucking others!"

Krislena cries out and whimpers as she feels him close behind. She begins to read as suddenly she feels something slipping around her throat, "Read It Krislena, show me how much you love my writing!"

She continues to read as her body feels the terror as the realization of a rope grips her ivory skin, trailing around her neck she lets go of the book with a slender hand to grasp the rope and pull it away from her neck, as survival mode kicks in. "I will fucking kill you after torturing your body as you tortured me all these months Krislena if you do not put both hands on that damn book of mine!" Krislena grabs the book again both hands sweating as the rope tightens around her neck, as her breath gives, and she convulses, as her hands both drop the book with only one motive to survive!

"You're a LIAR Krislena, look at you dropping MY BOOK to the floor! Is that all my book is to you? Trash? You promised me bitch!" The rope curls around her neck now as she rips fingernails to dig deeper in order to breathe as her flushed cheeks are mottled in terror and she begins to choke, saliva dripping down her chin, as her eyes roll back into her head.

She cannot breathe as she faintly hears him behind her whispering "You choked on me once with your lies and my book forgotten. You cannot review my book as you couldn't even start it for an aspiring author like myself!"

Life pours out of Krislena."How's that for a review Krislena?" Huh reader?

The TBR KILLER Leaves her forgotten!

ABOUT THE AUTHOR

KRISTI GUTHRIE

I'm currently living in Ga and work as a case manager in Mental Health! I love to escape into different stories and working on a novel plus collection of ten short stories!

My cats and kids deal with me 24/7 but I'm pretty awesome and my goals are WRITE ✍ Be Published & move to a nice little villa In FLA by the beach! My safe haven with your books and Mine!! Thank y'all for the support and all the love!

THE BIRTHDAY HOUSE

CHARLES HARNED

FINALIST

Context: Spooky Season | **Item:** Mirror

His phone's GPS lost signal three miles back, but Oliver didn't need it. His hands remembered the turns, even after two years. A ramshackle town that ended as fast as it started, and then the rental car's headlights swept across iron gates—rusted, half-open, perpetually waiting.

Mills-Blackwood House.

Even the name felt wrong in his mouth. Amelia had loved

it here, loved this decaying monument to someone else's grandeur tucked into the folds of southwest Virginia's Blue Ridge mountains, nearly flush with the Tennessee border. A haven of Antebellum decorum in everything from its crown molding to fixtures in an otherwise unruly, wild place. Every birthday, she'd insist they drive the four hours from Charlotte, her eyes bright with something he could never name.

"It speaks to me," she'd said once, running her fingers along the wallpaper's peeling edges. A maze of sepia and creaking floorboards. "Can't you feel it?"

He'd felt nothing but cold.

The house rose from the darkness like a shattered tooth—two proper stories of faded brick, narrow windows, and warped shutters, a sloping attic above it all. Massive oak trees pelting anyone brave enough to draw near with walnuts. Oliver killed the engine. The silence was immediate and total. No insects. No wind. Just the metallic pings of the rental car's heated engine contracting.

He shouldn't be here. Amelia was gone. The grief counselor said healing took time, that he'd know when he was ready to face memories. But last night, Amelia's thirty-fifth birthday, he'd dreamed of her standing at one of those narrow windows, a spidery palm pressed against the glass.

Waiting.

The key was where it always was, in a small jewelry box on a sideboard after he swung open the unlocked screen door. The inner door's lock resisted, then yielded with a groan that seemed to come from deep in the house's throat.

The interior smelled of mildew and something else—sweet and rotten, like flowers left too long in a vase. Oliver's flashlight beam cut through the darkness, illuminating room after room of gothic excess: the chandelier dripping with crystals, the mahogany staircase spiraling upward, the portraits of nameless Blackwood ancestors.

And the gilt mirror that turned the room into a circus horrorscape. Amelia had loved that mirror most of all.

His footsteps echoed as he climbed to the second floor, to the room where they'd always stayed. The tower room, his wife called it, though it technically wasn't a tower, just an octagonal room patterned with birds that looked more like bats in the shadows.

The bed was made, the moth-eaten quilt covered in dust. Oliver set his bag down and tried not to look at the empty space where Amelia used to sleep, curled on her side, smiling in the darkness.

"Why here?" he'd asked her once. "Why this place?"

"Because it remembers," she'd whispered. "Everything that happens here—it stays."

Hours crawled by. Oliver tried to read in the Gothic sitting room lined with dusty tomes, tried to sleep, but the house was too loud in its silence. The overbearing hum of memories he couldn't shake, all jumbled together and racing back and forth in his mind. All the words he wished he could say. So much his mind couldn't recreate even though he tried desperately to cling to every syllable passed between them. All of it fading all the time.

At midnight, he gave up and padded into the cavernous kitchen.

It was exactly as he remembered—the table too long, too ornate, arranged as if for a party that never came. She'd spend hours here, sitting in a wing-back chair, staring at nothing he could see.

Oliver sat in her place. The wood was unforgiving and cold. From this angle he could see into the long hallway that led to the back of the house. The hallway that had felt too dark, even with every light on.

Something moved at the end of it.

His breath caught. Just shadows, he told himself, playing tricks. But there was no light to create shadows.

The shape moved again, closer. The soft whisper of fabric against wood. Footsteps—light, familiar.

She emerged from the darkness, as if being born from it. Same long dark hair and flowing nightgown. Same knowing smile playing at her lips.

Her feet lost focus before they reached the floor. Her edges seemed to blur, to blend with the shadows.

"Oliver." Her voice was Amelia's but layered with something else, something that spoke from the walls themselves. "You came back."

He couldn't move. Couldn't breathe.

"I've been waiting." She drifted closer. "Every birthday. Every year. I told you this place remembers."

"You're not real." The words barely made it past his lips.

"I'm more real here than I ever was anywhere else." She

was right in front of him now, close enough that he should feel her warmth. “Don’t you understand? This is where I belonged. Where I’ve always belonged. The house knew it. I knew it.”

“Amelia, you—you died in a car accident.”

A long pause. “Did I? Or did I finally come home?”

Behind her, the hallway stretched impossible, endless. In its depths, other figures with blurred edges and empty eyes paced. All waiting. All watching.

“Stay with me,” Amelia whispered, and her voice was a chorus now. “It speaks to you too. I can see it. The house chose you the moment you walked through that door. It’s been waiting so patiently.”

Oliver tried to run, but his legs wouldn’t move. Amelia leaned closer, her face filling his vision, her black eyes reflecting infinite depths.

“Happy birthday to me,” she sang softly. “Happy birthday to me.”

And Oliver understood, finally, why she’d loved this place. Why she’d always smiled in the darkness. Why she brought him here, year after year, until the house knew his name.

The house did remember everything.

It could never forget.

ABOUT THE AUTHOR

CHARLES HARNED

Charles Harned was born in Galveston, Texas in 1992. He spent his youth in the Carolinas and graduated from Clemson University's business school in 2014. He finished his first novel in 2015, a mystery about a college fraternity gone bad. Since then he has written seven more novels running the gamut from mystery to topical thriller. He is the founder of Life9 Enterprises, a vertically integrated startup that seeks to influence the creative process from the initial manuscript through, ideally, film or television adaptation. Through Life9, Charles strives to champion writers and continues to amass a collection of highly marketable and adaptable commercial fiction.

charlesharned.com

THE ONE

DANIELLE HENNESSY

Context: Dating Disasters | **Item:** Photograph

Sarah added the finishing touches to her make-up and smiled at her reflection. With long brown hair, pale skin, and dark, sparkling eyes, she was truly a beautiful woman. As she gave her face a final check, her eyes flicked to the photograph tucked into the frame of the mirror.

"I think this might be it Kacey," she said to the girl in the photo. "I think I've finally found the one."

She let out a small, sad sigh as she continued to examine the photograph. With blonde hair, ice-blue eyes and rosy, pink lips, Kacey was the polar opposite in looks to Sarah. You would never guess that they were sisters. As different as they were in looks though, they were as similar in personality. With just a year between them, they shared everything from their clothes and shoes to their hopes and dreams.

Now it was just Sarah, navigating the world without her. Kasey had gone missing after a date - almost a year ago to the day. She had been found a few days later, beaten, broken and dumped naked into the local woodland. Arrests had been made but nothing had stuck, and Kasey's killer was still out there.

Sarah sniffed back her tears before she could ruin her make-up and, sliding the photograph into her handbag, she grabbed her keys and headed out to the restaurant. She was going on her first date with Liam who she had been talking to after connecting on a dating App.

Sarah had been about to give up looking for the one on the App completely after a string of bad dates, including one memorable disaster of a date that had turned up without any money, attempted to burp out the alphabet after downing a beer and then expected money for a cab after she told him he couldn't come home with her.

Liam seemed different though. For one, he had been happy to remain talking for a month before they actually had a date. Something most guys wouldn't have the patience for. Sarah was excited to finally meet him.

Arriving at the restaurant, she saw him waiting outside for her. She knew it was him because he looked exactly like his picture. *A good sign* she thought to herself. He greeted her with a hug and a friendly smile before leading her inside where they were seated in a cosy corner at a table lit by candles. They ordered their meals and the conversation flowed smoothly.

Liam was everything a guy on a first date should be. He was considerate, funny, and slightly flirty and to top it off, he was gorgeous. He felt too good to be true and when she told him this, he laughed and assured her that he had some skeletons in his closet. When they were done eating, he suggested they take a walk, and she agreed.

As she stood to leave, her elbow caught her bag and knocked it to the ground, spilling the contents. Liam helped her pick up her things, but when he picked up the photograph of Kacey, Sarah thought she saw him hesitate slightly, his eyes widening a fraction.

"Everything ok?" she asked nervously.

"Yeh..." Liam replied smoothly. "This girl just looks a bit like my sister" he said with a chuckle.

Sarah laughed with relief, "Well I hope it isn't, because that's my sister and that would be weird."

Liam chuckled again before passing her back the photograph and they left the restaurant together, falling back into an easy exchange as they walked. Lost in the conversation, Sarah didn't notice where they were until they reached the local woodland park. When she realised, she stopped abruptly.

"I can't be here," she stammered out. "We have to leave."

"Why would we do that when we're having so much fun," Liam smirked.

"You don't understand," Sarah begged. "I told you my sister died, but I didn't tell you she was murdered, or that her body was dumped here. I can't be here!"

"I know," Liam said, his tone dark and menacing. "I couldn't believe my luck when I saw that photograph. Two sisters in two years. That's the stuff dreams are made of!" he said with a sinister smile.

Sarah gasped as realisation hit before breaking into a run, diving into the trees for cover. It was cliché running forward instead of backwards towards people, but she figured she would have more cover to hide in the trees. Finding a patch of bushes that would both conceal her and give her a vantage point, she dived in and, heart pounding, strained her ears to listen. She could hear the snap of twigs as Liam stalked through the moon-lit woods.

"Come on out Sarah," Liam snarled. "Our date was going so well, and I have something special planned for you."

Sarah could hear him stalking closer and closer. Her breath caught in her throat. *This is it.* She thought to herself and wondered if Kacey had felt like this in her final moments.

Liam was close now. She heard him stop. She could hear his slow, steady breathing. Why had he stopped? Was she hidden enough?

"Got you!" Liam barked suddenly and Sarah felt his hands grip her tightly. She released a brief scream before he slammed a hand over her mouth.

"You're mine now," Liam sneered before frowning as he felt her shake her head and begin to laugh.

Sarah brought her hand up rapidly and buried the full length of the homemade nail file into his neck. Homemade because it had to be strong enough to pierce flesh.

As Liam fell to the ground gripping his neck, Sarah smiled down at him. "No..." she said triumphantly. "You're mine, and this is for my sister you asshole!"

Sarah watched as Liam took his last gurgling breath before placing the photo of her sister into his pocket. As she walked away, she whispered:

"I told you he was the one sis."

ABOUT THE AUTHOR

DANIELLE HENNESSY

I love books. I have done for as long as I can remember. I took a career break from my work in care in early 2024 to spend more time with my husband and three children and this has also given me the opportunity to dive headfirst into the world of writing, editing and, of course reading. I have edited several books now for other indie authors, I have read countless books and I even have a few half finished pieces of writing of my own but this is my first story to be finished and published which is very exciting. When I am not with my family or engaged in all things book related, I spend my time getting creative with various crafts and volunteering.

g goodreads.com/mrshennessy

POLICE EVIDENCE - #JK6V

MATT HEW

Context: Dating Disasters | **Item:** Diary

Thursday, 7th August 2025 - ***Late Shift***

CONSTABLE TYLER - CHARLIE 4

2210 hrs

En route - no speech emergency call, male voice heard asking for police no response to call taker, ended abruptly.

2218

Arrived.

2219

Nil persons observed, street empty. Target address: single story dwelling, nil lights on, single glowing red light in front left room. Curtains open. Nil occupants observed.

Two cars located in driveway:

- Vehicle 1 registration: RDP229 - BLACK FORD UTE
- Vehicle 2: FFG482 - BLUE TOYOTA HATCHBACK

2220

Making approach.

Nil answer to door knock. Nil answer to voice appeal.

Blood pool with drag mark observed through window.

2223

Call for shift supervisor (Sierra 1).

Backup requested.

Threat of grievous bodily harm.

Arming up.

Fire orders read and acknowledged.

2224

Making entry, Section 14 Search and Surveillance Act.

2235

1x male located in kitchen: deceased.

1x female located in bedroom: deceased.

On call detectives advised.

Scene locked down.

Control handed to shift supervisor Sergeant WALKER (Sierra 1).

Crime scene tape placed around house.

Scene guard front footpath.

SERGEANT WALKER - SIERRA 1

2223 hrs

Call from Charlie 4:

Blood observed in front window.

Making entry Section 14.

Enroute.

2235

Arrived.

Scene brief from Charlie 4.

1x male deceased - kitchen, face down, blood pool around body, drag marks from lounge, secondary pool in lounge.

1x female deceased - face up, bedroom floor, appearance of gunshot wound center forehead.

Delta 1, 2, 5, 6, 9 enroute.

Additional units requested.

Scene locked down.

2245

Delta 1 on scene - above scene brief given.

DETECTIVE SERGEANT GRANT - DELTA 1

2245 hrs

Arrived on scene.

Scene locked down - crime scene tape in place.

Ambulance staff on scene.

Sergeant in charge - SGT WALKER (Sierra 1).

Scene brief given.

2255

All detectives on scene.

Assignments:

- O/C Body - Delta 2,9
- O/C Scene - Delta 5,6

2257

Units making entry into scene.

2305

Initial scene description:

Single story dwelling unfenced front yard, 2 bedrooms - small wardrobes in each, 1 bathroom, 1 kitchen lounge area, small hall way, 2 linen cupboards, 1 detached carport, small backyard - fenced, No animals. 1 car parked under car port, 1 Car parked in driveway

Kitchen - Male approx 35yrs, 180cm tall, medium build. Signs of blunt force trauma to back of head. No ID on male.

1x Baseball bat located on floor next to male

Bedroom 1 - Female approx 34yrs, 175cm tall, small build. Single bullet wound to the head.

1x 9mm shell casing located to the right of the body.

1x iPhone next to the body, unlocked - placed in airplane mode - secured in an evidence bag.

2325

Crime scene technicians on scene.

Coroner on scene.

Friday, 8th August 2025 - *Early Shift*

DETECTIVE SERGEANT GRANT - DELTA 1

0915 hrs

Statement taken from Const. TYLER - ID 68941.

Recorded on DVD device 234.

0955

TYLER request Lawyer + Union rep.

Interview terminated after spontaneous admissions made.

Thursday, 7th August 2025 - *Night Shift*

DETECTIVE CONSTABLE SAMPSON - DELTA 5

2350 hrs

Bodies uplifted by Coroner.

All other units returned to base.

Scene handed to cleaners.

0158

Scene cleared returning to base to examine phone.

0218

Phone photographed.

Phone examination conducted with Delta 6.

Open applications - Facebook, Tinder, Messenger, WhatsApp, Candy Crush.

Message chain from 'Jack TYLER'.

Message chain from 'Dan FREEMAN'.

Overview from TYLER - Abusive and aggressive in nature, several threats to kill, nil further messages past 2200hrs 7 August 2025.

Overview from FREEMAN - Appears to be a new relationship, nil previous contact prior to 5 August 2025 - appears parties went on a date 7 August 2025.

Nil messages after 1830hrs - "Here".

Further inspection of messages from TYLER reveal previous intimate relationship spanning 5 months.

Profile of TYLER investigated.

0356

Phone brief with Delta 1.

Friday, 8th August 2025 - *Early Shift*

DETECTIVE SERGEANT GRANT - DELTA 1

1015 hrs

Interview restarted with Const. TYLER. Lawyer + Union rep present.

1218

Arrest of TYLER for murder x2.

Rights read as per aid memoir.

Do you understand your rights? Response - "Yes".

1316

Interview notes:

TYLER questioned re: messages sent to females phone. Admission made that he was the one to send them.

Question around his attendance at the address - GPS on vehicle shows he was at the address for 25 mins prior to initial call.

Question about blood under finger nail - Nil answered.

Question around 9mm police issued firearm - Nil answered.

Question about 1x round different to the standard issue firearm - Nil answered.

Question made around interactions with FREEMAN - became aggressive and admitted to hitting him on the head.

Further admission around stalking them while on date.

Advised him of his rights during initial interview - Lawyer requested - Interview terminated.

During second interview - Admissions made to discharge of firearm.

Further admissions to reasons - TYLER became aggressive - needed to be handcuffed to table to prevent harm to other parties in the interview.

1535

TYLER transported to the custody unit.

O/C Body to prepare court file.

1700

End shift.

ABOUT THE AUTHOR

MATT HEW

Matt is a police sergeant and recent convert to audiobook listener. He lives in New Zealand with his wonderful wife, who may or may not have penned this bio. When not sleeping, Matt can be found in his man cave, or working on the various projects and home renovations assigned to him by his aforementioned wonderful wife.

When asked whether Police Evidence - #JK6V was based on real events, Matt responded: No comment.

HALLOWEEN HAUNTING

RYLANNE HOLLOWAY

Context: Neighborhood Nightmares | **Item:** Mirror

You remember the stories you grew up being told, right?

The stories told in the dark, under the dense canopy of the woods or in the basement of your best friend's house that left you with chills up your arms and the hairs on the back of your neck raised.

You tried to convince yourself that the stories weren't real, that they were just made up from someone else's imagination, because they're all made up, right? Just told by camp counselors trying to scare children or stupid middle schoolers wanting to seem cool.

But what if I told you, those stories? They're actually true. Every single one of them.

It's Halloween, 2002, and you're sitting in the living room, peeking through the sheer linen curtains that hang over the windows. There's nothing but silence around you. Most nights, the streets of the neighborhood are busy, excited shrieks filling the air as kids play in the road and adults sit on their porches with cold beers in hand.

But tonight, trick or treating is already over, and all outside is quiet. The power on the street went out thirty minutes ago, forcing everyone into their homes and bolting doors behind them. Your parents aren't home - they somehow never are - and you keep glancing at the clock only to see the hands move slowly, *too slowly*. The minutes crawl by in the faint moonlight.

Why no one ever calls the police when it happens, you don't understand. But every year around Halloween, something happens. Something that takes a person from the neighborhood. And no one cares enough to get answers, not even the family members of the people who go missing. It's like everyone lives in a daze between Halloween every year, so the takings keep happening.

You tried to call the police once when you were thirteen after it happened, but when they came to your house to ask questions and interview neighbors, everyone seemed confused, unsure what you were talking about. The police left an hour later with questions that were quickly forgotten.

You also tried to leave one time, to run away, but the further you got from the street you grew up on, the worse the pain in your chest got, and you were forced to go back before your lungs collapsed in on themselves.

You don't understand what it is that happens every year, and you have no idea who to talk to about it. No one else acknowledges the disappearances that occur each Halloween. But you keep track. You always do.

This neighborhood, you know, is haunted.

A shadow slowly begins to grow on the sidewalk outside the window, and you quickly let the curtains fall.

There's a growl and a gargle of mucus as darkness grows closer. The Thing - it's here. You rear backward, watching its dark breath fog up the glass through the sheer curtains. You can't make out any distinct body parts, no matter how hard you look. Time freezes as you watch The Thing shift along the front of your house.

But before you can take your next breath, The Thing fades as it moves down the street, and your shoulders relax. Maybe you're safe. Maybe you won't be picked this year. But just in case, you dart down the hallway. The framed mirror you usually use to check your appearance flickers in your vision, but you refuse to look at it. You don't want to see how wide your eyes are or the sweat that beads your forehead. Your fingers tremble as you grab a knife from the kitchen. You don't think it will work on The Thing, but it gives you a feeling of protection. That has to be enough for now.

Certain it's gone, you hunch back in your spot on the couch and peek out the window, vigilant. You won't move again. It's too dark upstairs, the small windows facing opposite the moon making the rooms almost pitch black. Down here, though, you can see. There's only one way into the room, and from your spot on the couch, you can see the doorway in your periphery. If The Thing does come inside, you'll be ready.

A scream comes from outside, and you jump. It won't be you this year, it won't. That scream proved it, right? It picked someone else. You hear a door slam nearby, but you stay hunched in your spot. You know it's not safe until The Thing's shadow leaves the road, and it hasn't yet. It hovers over all the houses, shifting and expanding. It's still hungry.

A moment passes when a scuffle sounds in the kitchen, and you sit up, rigid. A hiss of breath grows louder. You turn your body to face the doorway as a smoky mist descends upon the room. You gasp and hold the knife up, a scream fighting to escape your throat. The mist pauses for a moment, almost listening to your struggle. Through the haze, you can barely, *just barely*, see a murky figure reflected in the mirror from the hallway. It towers toward the ceiling, a smoky fog swirling around the spot where its face should be. Your throat closes up, and The Thing continues moving toward you again, wrapping its tendrils around your body and squeezing tight. Before you can make a noise, darkness envelopes you, and the last sound you hear is the clatter of the knife hitting the floor.

ABOUT THE AUTHOR

RYLANNE HOLLOWAY

Rylanne Holloway is a recent MA graduate and avid reader from Tennessee. When she isn't teaching during the day, she's usually in her at-home library with her nose buried in a thriller or romance. Other published works include 'Stories of the Silenced and Mixed Media in Fiction: Disrupting Tradition for the Enhancement of Reader Experience.'

RUSH

MACHAELA JACKSON

Context: Neighborhood Nightmares | **Item:** Photograph

Autumn shoved me into the driver's seat and slammed the door shut. It hit my elbow hard and I clutched my arm to my body, gritting through my teeth. Maria slid in the back and Lynn got in the other back seat. I watched as Autumn walked around the trunk and sat next to me.

She flipped the mirror down and adjusted her rain-soaked hair, wiped some overapplied gloss from her lips, and turned to face me.

"Okay, Pledge. Drive."

"Drive… where?" I asked, hands tight on the wheel, knuckles turning white.

“Jesus, Sam… just DRIVE. Left.” Maria groaned.

“Okay, okay,” I conceded, backing out into the dark, dimlit street..

There was thudding coming from the back. The way back. The trunk.

Jenna was in the trunk. I could hear her yelling over the engine. The radio wasn’t running. No one had claimed the AUX.

My voice screaming in my mind;

Where are we going?

Is this all going to be okay?

What do they want us to do?

Was this a mistake?

“Stop worrying,” Maria laughed. “Breathe. This was me last semester… you’re fine. It’s okay.”

“… right.” I nodded, turning left onto a frontage road that led out of town.

We had been in the car for nearly fifteen minutes.

And it all went black.

I panicked as something covered my eyes, slamming on the brakes and clawing at the fabric.

“NO!” Autumn smacked my hand away. “Leave it. This is part of it. Tradition.”

“Tradition.” Lynn agreed.

My breathing quickened. Turning in Autumn’s direction, I pulled hard on the fabric. “Are you INSANE?? Do you want us to DIE?”

“Don’t be so damn dramatic,” Lynn laughed.

"I… I can't do this. What does this have to do with joining a stupid Sorority??? AND what about JENNA?"

Autumn rolled her eyes. "We've all been in the driver's seat and in the trunk, Sam. Don't be a whiny bitch. Drive or get out."

"And don't even bother coming back to the house." Lynn added.

"No entry for whiny bitches." Autumn laughed.

Maria had a small hint of regret in her eyes, though she didn't argue with her Sisters. "It's just a straight road, Sam. Just… drive."

I took a deep breath and pushed my back against the chair. My hands balled into fists on my lap as I clutched the bandana.

You need Sisters.

You need community.

You don't want to be all alone, do you? Stupid girl from a small town with no friends?

"… okay. Do it."

Autumn squealed and snapped open her Polaroid. The flash burned white against the dark. "Perfect!" she crowed, waving the photo as it slid out, the square frame already developing.

The bandana slipped just enough for me to see the road's faint double lines ahead, slick with rain. And for the first time, I felt something like pride. My grip steadied on the wheel. My foot pressed down on the gas. I could do this. I could prove myself. Their laughter filled the car, wild and sharp. It made me feel bold.

Then headlights appeared in the distance. Bright. Close. Too close.

Autumn's laugh turned into a shriek. Maria shouted my name. Lynn's nails dug into the back of my seat. My body froze. My reaction wasn't fast enough.

The van struck us head-on.

Metal crushed into metal. The world folded in on itself. My body whipped forward, then sideways. Glass tore at my skin. Screams split through the night, mine buried under theirs. The car rolled, again and again. The roof crumpled inward and the world went black.

When I opened my eyes, smoke curled from the crumpled hood. The windshield was a fractured star. Beside me, Autumn was slumped against the window, blood sliding down her temple. In the back, Maria and Lynn hung motionless, their heads bent at unnatural angles, their hair sticking to the shattered glass. The other vehicle was a mangled shadow in the rain. My hands shook as I unclipped my seatbelt. My knees buckled when I stepped into the night. The rain washed the blood from my arm, but it didn't wash away the image of their faces, still and broken.

I stumbled to the back, the trunk crumpled but still latched. My hands fumbled at the metal, slipping, trembling. When I pried it open, silence met me. Jenna lay twisted, eyes wide and glassy. The scream that built in my chest never made it out; it lodged there, burning.

The Polaroid camera sat in the grass, the flash bulb cracked but the photo still intact. I picked it up with shaking fingers. The five of us in the car; Autumn flashing a peace sign, Maria mid-laugh, Lynn pretending to be bored, me stiff as a statue. I dropped the camera, shoved the photo into my pocket, and stumbled toward the ditch, away from the wreckage.

When I woke, it was to the antiseptic brightness of a hospital room. Tubes, monitors, white sheets tucked too tight around me. My arm in a sling. My ribs screaming with every breath. The television mounted high in the corner flickered with the evening news.

"...a tragic loss for the East Side community. Four young women from Kappa Delta Sorority were killed late last night when their vehicle collided head-on with a family van during the storm. All passengers in both vehicles were pronounced dead at the scene. A small-town loss with far-reaching consequences. Police are still investigating what role hazing rituals may have played in the accident."

The screen shifted. A photo filled the frame. It had been taken a few hours before the they made me get in the car, lit by the Polaroid's flash. The anchor's voice pounded in my skull as she went on, "Police are still searching for the driver."

My pocket burned with the weight of the photo I had hidden away, the evidence that I was there. The only one left.

I closed my eyes and let the anchor's voice wash over me, steady as a heartbeat: *All dead. All but one.*

ABOUT THE AUTHOR

MACHAELA JACKSON

Machaela Jackson is a wife and mother of four from Wisconsin. She has three books published and is always working on the next project on her list.

With two degrees in education, Machaela works for a nonprofit where she teaches adult immigrants the English language.

THE H.O.A.

AMANDA JOSEPHINE

SECOND PLACE WINNER

Context: Neighborhood Nightmares | **Item:** Scissors

Afternoon: Back Porch

My fucking neighbor is an asshole. A useless piece of shit. This used to be a nice, peaceful street. Quiet. A place where you could sit on your porch with a cold drink and wave at your neighbors as they pushed strollers, rode bikes, or took evening walks. It was that way until Daryl moved in, three years ago. Daryl is what we like to call at the HOA meetings "a loser." He doesn't have a job. He sued a supermarket for not having a wet floor sign, won, and ended up here. He constantly causes disturbances with his music blasting at full volume.

I have resided in this neighborhood for 25 years. My husband and I raised our two sons here. We have annual BBQs in the cul-de-sac. Everyone watches out for each other. That is, until Daryl and his big speakers and rap music. He works on cars in the driveway, with his ass hanging out, and blasts that god-awful noise anytime he's outside - which can be for hours.

I am sitting on my porch trying to write. I stare at my laptop with the words "Chapter One" heading up an otherwise blank Word document. The music makes it impossible to focus, and I have to get started on this book. *Thump. Thump.* The music's bass rattles my teeth. I slam my laptop lid shut. Something has to be done. The cops have been no help. "If we don't see it, ma'am, there's nothing we can do." The last officer who came out told me. What a fucking joke! We will discuss it again at the HOA meeting tonight. I go back inside my house, shutting the sliding glass door, which does nothing to muffle the sound.

That Night: HOA Meeting

The HOA meeting takes place at the president's house. There are about six of us in attendance. People can't sleep. Can't put their babies down for a nap. Everyone is on edge and snappy. Couples have been arguing more, and kids are bickering. People are at their wits' end.

"You never know what time of day or night he'll start playing it or when he'll turn it off," I hear Karen, my across-the-street neighbor say to Marie, her next-door neighbor.

"I know, it's ridiculous. Steve hasn't slept in days. He's working the night shift and with that noise..." Marie trailed off; she didn't need to finish.

I took my seat beside Mike, an older guy who lived on the other side of Daryl. Mike's wife, Carley, was here tonight too, a sweet, grandmotherly woman. She used to bake my boys cookies. I smile at them, and they nod in return. Laura, the HOA president, calls the meeting to order, and immediately, everyone starts talking at once. Yelling their complaints about Daryl.

Laura tries to regain control of the meeting and finally resorts to blowing a gym whistle to get everyone's attention.

"I know everyone is frustrated. I am too. Mitch can't sleep. The baby won't take a nap. We're all so exhausted," Laura addressed the group. "I feel like I'm losing my mind."

"Carley's blood pressure has been elevated for the last month, the doctors can't get it under control," Mike said, his voice catching with emotion. "This has gone beyond just being annoying."

Mumbles of agreement arose from my neighbors. They continued to voice their complaints, getting louder, tears were flowing, and their angry voices kept climbing in volume. "What if we killed him?" Someone suggested. The room fell into dead silence. It felt like no one was breathing. Then someone chuckled quietly, and others joined in.

"That's ludicrous, right? We can't do that...can we?" Marie asks, looking to the rest of us, her eyes pleading.

"I mean, we'd get arrested, right?" Karen inquired, laughing awkwardly. Mike stood up, lifted his head, and looked each of us directly in the eye.

"We have to do this. This is affecting my wife's health and everyone's mental health too. We can't stand for that," he shook his head, taking a deep breath. "I can take care of it myself, no need for everyone to get involved. If I go down for this, just promise me you all will take care of Carley."

The room was stunned. There was an unspoken agreement between us. We would let this happen. As we all turned to go home, the sound of blaring music filled the room.

Midnight: The Neighborhood

I am trying to wrap a present for my son and listen to some jazz. I can't hear my music over Daryl's speakers. I snap. I grab my good scissors from the table - the ones that slide seamlessly through the paper. I march across the yard. His back is to me, his ass crack hanging out like always. I jump on his back and stab the scissors into his carotid artery. The blood spurts out, covering my hands and face. It feels warm and sticky as it sprays. He throws me off his back onto the hard pavement. He looks down at me, eyes wide. I smile at him as he throws his hand up to cover the wound, but it's too late. He falls, his blood running across the driveway.

I stand up and look down at him. His fat, hairy stomach protrudes over his waistband. Gross. His brown eyes are glazed over with death, and his mouth hangs open, tongue protruding. I walk to the stereo and flip the switch to off. On my way home, I reach down and grab my scissors, yanking them from his neck. These are my best pair. I drop the bloody weapon into the pocket of my robe and walk across the yard.

I see my neighbors standing on their porches, watching. They slowly go back inside their houses and shut their doors, turning off the lights.

I couldn't let a sweet old man like Mike go down for murder. After all...I'm the one who suggested it.

ABOUT THE AUTHOR

AMANDA JOSEPHINE

Amanda Josephine is an indie author and Licensed Professional Counselor who spends her days helping others and her nights crafting dark, twisty tales. Her debut short story, Deadly News, appeared in Killer Thrillers: The Anthology, Volume 1. The winner of the 2025 Anthology of the Year in the Bookstagram Awards. Her second story, The Devil's in the Details, was featured in Vacay & Decay: Vacation Nightmares.

Amanda also earned 2nd place in the 1000 Word Thriller Challenge for her short story The H.O.A.. Her debut novel, The Puzzle, is set to release in late 2026.

Amanda lives in the beautiful Blue Ridge Mountains of Virginia with her supportive husband, teenage son, and their beloved Boxer. When she's not writing or reading, you can find her exploring new places, soaking up the fall weather, cheering for her favorite hockey team, or, more often than not, buying more books than she has shelf space for.

THE MAZE

TANYA KOLB

THIRD PLACE WINNER

Context: Spooky Season | **Item:** Broken Phone

I slowly made my way back onto my front porch just before dawn, the old wooden swing creaked its familiar creak as I sat down. The feel of the cool Autumn breeze and twinkle of the stars settled my nerves. Over 40 years, I'd lived in this old house on the hill. Most of those were happy years. Tonight, I closed the books on another Halloween. It may very well be my last. You think about things like that when you get to be a man my age. My sweet Mazie used to love Halloween. For her, it wasn't just a holiday. She's been gone almost 10 years now, though. I can't help but think of all of those weeks that she'd spend planning those famous haunted mazes that she loved so much. Every little detail had to be perfect. I wasn't much of a fan of the holiday myself, but oh how I loved the joy it brought to her. I would have done anything for that woman. I still would, if I could.

Living back off the main road, at the top of the mountain had its advantages when you had a love for the spooky season. At least that's what Mazie always used to say. She would meticulously build her haunted maze behind our house every year. It would butt up to the fence along the cliffs. She would bark orders at me, and I would happily comply. For years, people came in droves to walk through there and be scared out of their minds. I could barely hear the crashing waves for their screams and laughter. Our town was small, and the locals didn't pay us much attention. Most of the kids came from neighboring towns. The numbers started dwindling as the years went by and we grew older. My precious Mazie just wasn't able to do things like she used to do and honestly neither was I. I would have given her the world, if I could have. I started to see a sadness creep into her.

I feel that sadness now. A longing for the years that have long since passed me by. Things that I can't get back no matter how bad I want to. I remember how the teenagers started to sneak up here to the hill on Halloween, years after there was no longer a maze to run through. They came for meanness. They came looking for a different kind of fun. They started out, in those first couple of years, by throwing toilet paper in the trees and leaving trash on the lawn. It would take me all the next day to clean it up while Mazie cried quietly in the house. I knew her heart was breaking. Over the years, they graduated from toilet paper to breaking windows and slashing tires. We became the crazy old couple on the hill. Our new holiday ritual was locking the doors and keeping the lights off on Halloween night. While Mazie cried upstairs, I sat silently at the front window watching.

I lost her in the spring. The birds were singing, and all of her flowers were in bloom. There wasn't a cloud in the sky that day. I went to wake her up and she looked so peaceful, too peaceful. Something in me just broke. It had been just the two of us. Now, I was alone. I became the crazy old man in the haunted house on the hill. Mazie would have been so proud. The way that most people were afraid of this house. I believe it would have brought a smile back to her face, one that I hadn't seen in years. Oh, how I loved that smile. I even started to look forward to Halloween myself. This year was going to be great.

I started early, in late August, as soon as I felt the first cool winds start to blow. I was so excited to set up the maze. I had been planning it in my head for months. I carefully made my way up to the dusty, stifling attic and pulled down years' worth of mechanical monsters and props. It took me months to set them up. Being in my 70's definitely didn't help. Halloween night, I sat on my porch and waited.

As the night grew darker, I watched as the pranksters snuck into the yard. A little smile would cross my lips each time they would notice the small lighted sign that simply read "haunted maze, this way". Each one let their curiosity get the better of them as they followed the path around to the back of the house. There would be the occasional scream or gasp or the flicker of a cell phone and I'd grin to myself and think of Mazie. I couldn't help but think that she was smiling down on me. Several of them came through as the night wore on. There would be no property damage tonight. "Well, Mazie" I said, "we finally had another successful year."

I got up from my dark seat on the porch around 4 a.m. and headed around to the back of the house. The maze was a tall one this year. The tallest that we'd ever had. It towered over the fence along the cliffs. I walked carefully to where the maze ended, mindful not to fall over the edge myself. I needed to make sure that nothing would ever be found. There could be no evidence. As I peered over the edge of the cliffs, at the maze's end, I counted 5 broken and battered bodies. Each one twisted into its own unique and deformed shape. No one would ever find them, and they wouldn't be back to torment me next year. The waves would soon wash them away. As I turned to walk back to my house, I spotted a broken cell phone. I turned it over in my hands, shrugged my shoulders, and tossed it over the side.

ABOUT THE AUTHOR

TANYA KOLB

Tanya lives in rural South Carolina. She is married with 5 children, 1 grandchild, and 2 dogs. She spends her time reading and thinking about writing stories. She loves Halloween and all things scary. The Maze is her first attempt at writing since college (which was many moons ago!)

THE MIRROR KNOWS WHICH ONE

CHARLENE MATTSON

Context: Spooky Season | **Item:** Mirror

There was a piece of playground equipment which, when two people stood at either one, allowed them to communicate across the length of the park. Bryony, eight years old and already acutely aware of her own loneliness, hated it, but would still stand at one of the speaking tubes and tentatively utter an unanswered greeting.

She wasn't sure why she continued this ritual. It felt like someone was waiting to answer her, so she sent out her greeting, but it was to no avail. She glowered at the speaking tube and headed for the slides.

At home, Bryony lay on her bed and waved up at her

reflection in the long mirror. No one knew why the landlord put a mirror on the ceiling, though some of her parents' friends stared at it and started giggling. Her dad tried to take it down when she was quite young, but she cried and it stayed.

It was *sort* of like having a twin sister. At least it was someone to talk to. Sometimes she remembered two voices crying for the mirror to stay, but she was pretty sure she imagined it. It had always been just her and her loving if distant parents.

Other than the mirror, the other thing that no one was allowed to touch was the carved wooden box on the fake mantle piece over the equally fake fireplace. It was a small box carved all over with lilies and roses. She had once run her fingers over it in a small fit of childhood rebellion but then she felt strangely sad and stopped.

Halloween meant fun school activities at the park. Excited children played on the slides and climbed the bars. Bryony glared at the speaking tubes but maintained her ritual, not expecting anything in return.

"Hello," came a voice in return to her usual greeting.

Jolted, she looked up, but there was no one at the other end. She narrowed her eyes. *"Who's there?"*

"Who?"

She shook her head. It must have been an echo. She flounced in her princess costume back to her teacher. One of her classmates squeaked at a scratched and distorted mirror seemed to reflect a girl screaming silently at the young boy. No one believed him and he tried to show one of the supervisors, she only saw herself.

Once home, she lay on her bed and looked up at her reflection. It looked a little different somehow: the pink dress more rumpled, her brown hair limper. She frowned and the reflection frowned too, but slightly out of sync. She rolled out of bed and brushed herself off, ready to go out into the fog to collect candy.

In the mist, the playground took on a sinister air and Bryony wanted to avoid it. But she steeled her spine and sauntered through in front of her father. She was just passing the equipment when the reflection from the battered play mirror caught her eye. She assumed it was just her, caught in the glow from a lone streetlight, but the face looked twisted. She shuddered and ran away. Her father frowned, pulled out his phone to text his wife, and followed his daughter as she pelted up the small hill back to familiar neighbourhoods.

When they returned home, Bryony had largely forgotten about what she had seen in the park and was happily sorting through her candy in her room, eating every other one.

Tap.

Tap. Tap.

She looked around. The noise seemed to be coming from

the ceiling. She looked up to see her face staring back at her, but then her reflection's hands rose up and slammed against the mirror. *Bang!*

She screamed and to her relief, her parents burst into her room and held her close. She tried to tell them about the mirror, but when they all looked up, there was nothing to be seen but themselves. But the little girl in their circle of arms winked at her and then her face seemed to slide and melt away. She buried her face into her father's shoulder and then they put her to bed. She rolled over so that she couldn't see her reflection smiling down at her.

When she finally fell asleep, two figures returned to her room, surrounded her bed with thick red and black candles. Their smoke wreathed the room, silver in the moonlight. She shifted uneasily in her sleep as familiar low voices slithered into her dreams, snaring her mind and soul and lifting it up until it was locked behind silver and glass. The candles blew out and the little girl in the bed sighed and fell into a deep sleep, a smile on her face.

Morning dawned, the first of November. The little girl yawned, stretched, and frowned; she'd had uneasy dreams all night and whisps of them chased her into the day. She scowled slightly at the bucket of candy by her bedside, figuring that the sugar may have caused the nightmares. She went downstairs where her parents were waiting with breakfast.

Her reflection in the bedroom ceiling obediently followed her out of sight.

"Good morning, Bianca darling," her mother said, kissing her forehead. She ate her breakfast and went to the living room. Her parents were out of sight, and she ran her fingers over the engraved lily and rose box on the mantle.

"Thank you for keeping them company, Bryony," she whispered to it. "It's my turn now. Rest behind the mirror."

ABOUT THE AUTHOR

CHARLENE MATTSON

Charlene Mattson is a northern British Columbia BC author of horror and mystery/fairy tale retellings. She also enjoys baking, gaming, and walking in the woods. She is currently doing a Master of Education focusing on adult learners. She has two children, both of whom inspire stories, two cats and a dog who are less useful in the writing process but try their best.

WITHIN THE DARKNESS

ISABELLA MCDANIEL

Context: Dating Disasters | **Item:** Broken Phone

"Why!?!" I screamed, the forest consuming my pleas as soon as they left my mouth.

I had been in the forest for days. It all started on an anniversary camping trip. I pulled out my almost-useless phone, which was broken during a fight. Through the cracks, I could see there was a message from my best friend Amber, but all I got to read was, 'Aster???' before my screen went blank as the last bit of charge was used up.

After spending days in the woods, you realize how suffocating it can be, the empty air hanging heavily all around. Tears rolled down my cheeks, thinking back to when Gale and

I were happy, when all we could think about was each other. That was before the betrayal.

I took off my backpack and sat on the ground, wondering how long he had been lying about everything. Gale had been having a secret affair behind my back with my best friend, leaving me alone, thinking he had just been working late. Every time I think about it, my head starts spinning out of control. I take a deep breath, calming myself, and start rummaging through my backpack.

"There must be something in here I can eat..." I mutter, my stomach growling loudly at the mention of food. There was nothing; my hunger remained.

The forest was thick with trees and a slight undergrowth, glowing with the colors of fall. The leaves were so dense that I couldn't see the sky, but I could tell it was late in the day. Visibility was getting worse by the minute. I got back up to continue searching for any signs of civilization when I heard a crunching sound behind me.

"Gale? Is that you?" I asked into the unsettling darkness around me. The crunching stopped for a moment before continuing again. I followed the noise this time, farther into the darkness ahead. An enormous tree stood there, casting ominous shadows over me as the sun sank behind it.

I walked around the tree, still following the noise. A liquid was pooling around the roots of the tree, discolored in the darkness. I looked up. Slowly. A dark figure was hanging above me, its shape distorted. I knelt to find my flashlight in the side pocket of my backpack. I clicked it on, and it flickered for a moment as I aimed it above my head. When my eyes focused, I could see Gale, his body mutilated and bleeding from multiple wounds. He reached his butchered hand toward me before going limp, a last breath shuddered, and he was gone. The crunching continued.

The tree was slowly, but visibly, twisting around him. Before I could react, I felt an earthy root twisting around my ankle. I screamed, dropped my flashlight, and lost any visibility I could have hoped for. Dropping to the ground, I scrambled to get away, but the grip just got tighter around my ankle. In a desperate attempt to regain my freedom, I turned and bit the root, it recoiling as the wood splintered between my teeth.

Its grip loosened, and I had my chance. I used all my strength to launch myself off the ground and run as fast as I could. Low-hanging branches hit me at every turn. I heard branches breaking behind me. I didn't have time to stop; I just had to get away. I ran until I could hear the forest quiet itself again.

I wandered for what seemed like hours, following the sound of running water and walking slowly to be able to hear if the forest came back to life. As I got closer to the sound of the water, I smelled something; something tangy, something familiar.

As I continued walking, the darkness was slowly becoming less dense, as if there was a hole in the treetops glowing with moonlight. Then I found it, a small area with clear skies in which I could see the stars dotting the darkness above.

I walked cautiously into a small clearing, and a foul odor hit me like a ton of bricks. It was overwhelmingly metallic, with a hint of decay. I had smelled it a thousand times before as an emergency responder. Blood.

I looked around the clearing, and everything was still discolored in the remaining darkness. The ground squished under my feet, soggy with more blood than I had ever seen in one place.

The crackling started again, and before I could move, there was a strong grip on my leg, sweeping my feet out from underneath me. I was hanging upside down by one leg, as large branches encased my body, wrapping tighter and tighter. When I tried to scream, a large branch launched itself into my mouth, squirming its way down my throat, cutting against my esophagus. I gagged, and blood dripped from my mouth. I coughed violently as the branch split apart to invade my stomach and my lungs next.

Tears poured down my splitting face, and blood spilled everywhere as my cheeks tore open, and relentless pain hit me. My mind raced. Had Gale planned this?, I wondered if, having cheated on me, it was possible. My eyes were close to bursting out of my head, the branch getting larger the farther it went into my body. I could no longer breathe. I struggled, pained gags erupted from my mouth as my throat, my esophagus, and my vocal cords were demolished. With a wet "squelch," my eyes popped out of their sockets, leaving me blind in my last moments of utter peril.

The clearing fell into an uncomfortable quiet as the final

crunch of my bones echoed throughout the forest. Blood, bones, and splinters of wood littered the clearing. A mess of branches hung over the edge of the clearing, still dripping with my remains. An eerie stillness crept in as the forest lay in wait for its next unsuspecting prey.

ABOUT THE AUTHOR

ISABELLA MCDANIEL

I am a high schooler and I love writing horror stories/ reading horror stories! I live on a farm so I don't have a lot of free time but I do have a special connection with plants and wildlife which is why I wrote about the forest!

facebook.com/isabella.mcdaniel.960086
tiktok.com/@lisamcdaniel09

THE WARD

PETE MONCRIEFF

Context: Spooky Season | **Item:** Diary

2024

The hospital window was covered in mold —greenish, black, disgusting mold.

As Paul lay in bed, he could barely see anything in the room. It was dark, and a tall box occupied a corner. A gloomy light in the darkness passed the window; at least it seemed dim. He couldn't really tell; the window was so dirty. Didn't anyone clean them?

He felt nauseous. Had he eaten or drunk something that disagreed with him? Paul had a distant memory of having eaten something the night before. He couldn't remember where he had been, or what it was. He vaguely remembered something.

A tall, dark figure with a sinister energy stood at the door.

Standing there, listening as Paul laid there quietly and tried not to make any noise.

Why was the figure there?

Who, or even what was it?

Again, Paul felt his eyes close. As he began to fade, he heard a loud groan. He woke with a start.

Nothing.

Was it even still night?

Outside the window, the light he had seen previously was still on and softly glowing. The difference now was that it was gently swaying. Paul realized that there was a breeze blowing. Through the mold, he could just about make out a tall building.

A large, somber building.

Suddenly, he heard another thundering moan; The odd presence was still in the corridor outside his room.

What had he heard? Was it genuine? Was there really something out there?

Once again, the atmosphere surrounding him became dull, and he fell into a deep, disturbed sleep. He began to dream; the window looking outside was brighter, although still quite dirty. The light he saw when he was awake still shone, although he only saw the small bulb that was nearly out, he didn't understand why it still burned.

He remembered that he was still dreaming and glanced at his watch. The time was accurate.

He woke up.

Paul got out of bed and tiptoed towards the door. He remembered that a figure had previously been there.

It was gone.

Where it had been, a rotten smell lingered. It was almost as if a stagnant pond was there in its place, but without the water. The stench was overpowering and made Paul feel quite faint.

What was it, this evil-smelling apparition? Was it something real, or was it part of the dream world?

The thought scared him.

As he stood at the door, he listened intently to the noises that he heard. The groan was soft, but further away now. There was also a loud, but persistent shuffle. Was the sound something to do with the human shape he had seen before?

Paul was scared; he felt cold and completely covered in goosebumps. As he walked back to the bed on which there now lay a book, the year on the cover was 1923.

He opened the small book, which he deduced was a diary. Inside the front cover was a handwritten letter.

If you find this after I am gone, please read. I beg you to be careful. Please?

Take care, Samuel.

The following day's page had a drawing; he recognised the building he was in, but it seemed as if there might be a tunnel between that building where he was and the tall building outside. The next few days' entries went on to describe how the codes could be cracked for the various rooms inside the tower. Each day, the writer of the diary discovered a new room and deduced how to get in.

Paul pocketed the diary and left the room stealthily. He looked both ways and saw nothing. There was nothing to hear either. Not a breath, nor a growl or roar could be heard. The silence was eerie; it was almost as if something was listening and watching.

What was waiting? Paul shrugged.

Then that smell came again.

Before he continued, he took another look at the diary. The next day must have been one where the owner (his name was a bit foggy. Sam; was it?) had managed to reach another room.

Paul strolled down the corridor, his footsteps quietly echoing as he went.

He turned left and ambled past several more locked, possibly sealed, doors, ones that he didn't have the codes for entry. Eventually, he reached the end of the corridor down which he had felt he had been walking all day. He'd really only been moving for the best part of an hour.

This must be the other building.

Here, he stopped: One, because it seemed that he couldn't go further; two, because it was almost pitch black; and three, he thought he could hear breathing coming from somewhere quite close to him.

Soon, he saw a flashing light, but where it originated was not easy to ascertain. The light was as small as a pinprick.

Then another. And another.

Even more appeared revealing the outline of… a doorway?

Paul stopped and thought. What had happened to the apparition?

He remembered the disgusting stench from the other building, but did that mean that whatever or whoever had been following him was only there and couldn't get over here? He began to wonder if what he had seen over there had really been a ghost?

He looked in the diary. The final entry depicted a door (maybe this one). Beside the drawing of the door and the lights was a final panel. The writing beside it instructed the reader to move forward.

Paul did as the book asked. As he did, he collapsed.

As he did so, he felt himself being caught. A young boy had seized him with the help of an old man.

"Grandpa Frank! Grandpa Frank! We caught one! What do we do now?"

The tall, shadowy, disgusting-smelling man and the boy

took hold of Paul and shuffled toward the door. As they walked, all three slowly disappeared.

Quietly, a voice could be heard in the distance:

"Thank you, Samuel. We can do a lot with this."

The year on the cover was 1925.

IF YOU FIND THIS AFTER I AM GONE, PLEASE READ IT. I BEG YOU TO BE CAREFUL. PLEASE!

TAKE CARE, PAUL.

ABOUT THE AUTHOR

PETE MONCRIEFF

I emigrated to the US 5 years ago and live with my husband. My time is taken up looking after 2 cats and Atticus, he's also a cat but we're sure he thinks he's a dog. In my spare time I can be found sitting at a piano or on a roller coaster.

THE WITCH OF SALEM

T. A. PALMER

Context: Spooky Season | **Item:** Diary

Tik tock, tik tock, tik tock

Thump thump thump thump thump thump

Bring me back, Angelina.

Angelina snapped out of her trance. She looked at the black cat clock on the wall where the eyes moved back and forth on each second; she put her hand on her chest and felt her racing heartbeat. A few deep breaths eased her nerves, and she went back to reading her book on witchcraft. She owned a small novelty store in Salem, Massachusetts, specializing in the eerie and creepy: potions, old books, stuffed spiders and black cats, witch hats, and anything that would attract tourists into her store.

It was October 1st, the leaves had started to turn orange and fall to the ground, pumpkin farmers were harvesting their crop, and the town was putting up their Halloween decorations. This year was particularly special, it was going to be a full moon on Halloween, which only occurs once every nineteen years. Hotels had been sold out for close to a year, special events and haunts had been planned, and actors were hired to roam the city and scare the shit out of the visitors.

The shop door opened, and an older lady entered. She shuffled up to the counter—her wiry grey hair covering her eyes, she set a book on the counter.

"It's time to bring her back, Angelina."

Angelina tilted her head trying to place the woman who seemed to know her, "I'm sorry, do I know you?"

"Do you have the time dear?" The woman asked, ignoring Angelina's question.

Angelina glanced up at the cat clock, "It's three," she started to say, but the woman was gone. All that was left as proof that she was there was the book she had set on the counter. It was very old and fragile, bound in calfskin. Curious, Angelina opened it. There was a folded piece of paper inside. Angelia unfolded and read the letter.

Angelina,

This is the diary of Tituba, the first witch of Salem—your ancestor. Its contents will guide you in how to bring her back.

"My ancestor? What in bloody Hell?"

Angelina locked the door and turned the open sign to closed. She went back to the diary and started reading. As she read, whispers of the past entered her ears. The stories of the little girls echoed off the walls. This wasn't one of Angelina's trances, this was happening. She read of the girls' possessions—a potion, meant to turn the girls into Tituba's slaves in this life and the next: cursed water, egg whites of three snake eggs, one drop of dart frog venom, and three drops of Tituba's blood.

The potion was working, but the priest was my better, countering my potion with the words of God.

Angelina read on, mesmerized by the words written by Tituba's hand. The more she read, the more her demeanor changed. She felt hate and anger that wasn't there before. The last entry depicted only by the year 1692 was an incantation. One final spell. Angelina sat back confused, "She wasn't killed during the trials. She was released. So why does it stop here?"

As she contemplated the answers to her own questions, a knock at the door caught her attention. A middle-aged woman stood at the windowed-door and pleaded to be let in.

She's the one. Let her in.

The voice glided Angelina to the door; she didn't recall taking a step. The thumping in her chest returned. Sweat dampened her hair and palms. The giggles of little girls played in Angelina's ears. Her hate and anger amplified. She reached for the lock and turned it.

"Oh, thank you. I thought you closed at five. I just need to pick up the book I ordered. You called me yesterday to tell me it was in."

"Yes, of course. Mrs. Parris, right? Please, follow me," Angelina continued. "It's just in the back room here. Come."

Mrs. Parris followed Angelina to the back room and the door slammed shut behind her on its own. Mrs. Parris, startled by the loud noise, turned to look at the closed door. Angelina grabbed the closest blunt object she could reach—a ceramic pumpkin and smashed it on Mrs. Parris' head. Mrs. Parris collapsed to the floor unconscious.

When Mrs. Parris came to, she was strapped to a table. She tried to scream out but couldn't. Angelina was in the middle of the incantation in the diary that was resting Mrs. Parris's breasts.

"...Spirit of death, take this soul of the living and free from the side of Satan sister-witch Tituba."

The entire incantation was repeated over and over. Thunder could be heard crashing outside. The walls started vibrating; vials shook from the shelves and crashed to the floor. A dark cloud formed above Mrs. Parris's body; her eyes rolled back into her head and mouth was agape. The clear spirit of Mrs. Parris was pulled from her body, the black cloud replacing it. Angelina kept focus on the words, blood now running from her nose. Little girl voices echoed the incantation in the small room. Angelina finished the spell for the tenth time, energy erupted from the body, and blew Angelina backward, crashing into the wall behind her.

Angelia slowly rose to her feet and walked over to the still body on the table. She rested her hand on its forehead. It was cold to the touch, but the body temperature slowly rose. The eyes snapped open and full orbs of solid black stared at Angelina—a smile finally formed.

"I'm back," Tituba stated, as pupils returned to her eyes.

Tituba looked at the ropes that held her to the table and they loosened without a word. She sat up and took Angelina's face in her hands, "Thank you, my dear. We have a lot of work to do before the full moon. I will have my revenge!"

ABOUT THE AUTHOR

T. A. PALMER

I am currently a visually impaired student at Central Michigan University majoring in history and creative writing. I started my college journey at the age of 49 and am in my final year. I have always enjoyed writing in multiple genres and plan on continuing after graduation. I enjoy theatre, museums, and football.

VALENTINE'S DAY DISASTER

CRICKET PEHLEMANN

Context: Dating Disasters | **Item:** Candle

I can't wait to see Pablo when I get off work today to enjoy our first Valentine's Day together, one that neither of us will ever forget. I have a few errands to run before going home to start cooking the lasagna. Everything has to be perfect.

I am so nervous. Pablo is the sweetest guy and doesn't mind that I have two daughters. He invites them on our dates to dinner and the movies. He seems to be vested in this relationship as much as I am. He even invited us to meet his parents for dinner and drinks afterwards to get to know us better. His parents didn't speak English fluently, but it wasn't hard to understand one another and know they approved of us.

I drive to the flower shop to pick up the fresh rose petals I ordered last week and give them the address to send a black rose to my ex as it's our anniversary of... our end. I drop the girls off at my BFF's for a few hours, as she has a date later this evening. I want Pablo and I to enjoy the evening first, if you know what I mean. I go to the store for last minute candles and the forgotten Parmesan cheese for the garlic bread.

I open the door and enter my two-bedroom apartment, close the door and take a deep breath while leaning against the door. Pablo will be here soon. He wants to finish working on his car. Why did he pick Valentine's Day to change the oil and wash his Cuda? I can't concentrate on that now; I need to make sure everything is absolutely beautiful.

I start with cooking the lasagna, boil the noodles, fry the sausage and hamburger while my award-winning sauce is simmering on that back burner. It smells amazing.

I check the remaining items on my to-do list to gauge timing.

- vacuum 10 minutes
- Lasagna 1 hour
- Pour the wine, add strawberries 2 minutes
- Giftbag 5 minutes
- Garlic Bread 8-10 minutes
- Salad 2 minutes

- Light Candles - when arrives
- Clean sheets on bed 5 minutes
- Set table with plates, silverware, cheese plate, server knife 2 minutes

Pablo calls to say he is almost here. Oh boy, my heart is beating fast. I look around, make sure it's perfect. I spread the rose petals leading from the front room and down the hallway to my bedroom where I place the remaining petals in a heart shape. Corny, I know.

I hear his car rumbling, as he parks outside my apartment door. It sounds amazing. I quickly light the candles while he's exiting the car. Pablo approaches the door and knocks impatiently on the door as if he's been standing outside for an extended period of time. I open it to find him empty handed. I am not high maintenance, truly, but come on, a little something would be nice.

Pablo looks around, sees all my hard work and says... "I feel sorry for the next girl."

What the actual... ? "What do you mean? Next girl?" I am shattered.

"You know. You did it all. How is *she* going to compete with this? She has big shoes to fill."

In this very moment, I realize the relationship is going nowhere and will never be the same again. My breaking heart. I will not pour my heart into something that isn't spilling back to me. Sure, he loves my girls, but it isn't enough.

He obviously doesn't care if he is worried that I ruined it for the next girl.

I turn and walk to the table. I motion to his seat as I sit. I don't even know what to say. I am completely dumbfounded. I am half listening, but nod when he talks about everything new the car has. Then he says, "Sorry I didn't stop to get you a card...work on my car. I almost didn't come, but I know you want to spoil me, so I came. It's really good. You out did yourself."

"I sure did." I say. He looks up at me and grabs his gift, a giftbag full of Prince memorabilia, his second obsession.

"No, really, you out did yourself. I feel bad, all this for me; I just didn't have time to stop, like I said."

"It doesn't matter. You do know that they sell cards prior to Valentine's Day, not just on Valentine's Day?!"

"Yeah. Sorry."

My phone rings and my sitter asks if Pablo is here yet. I say yes, he is and she could bring the kids home now. She hears my tone and knows it isn't good.

"Oh good, the girls are coming home now? I can't wait to see them."

"I need to get them ready for bed." I answer as I walk into the kitchen for more bread.

Pablo is oblivious and yet knows something is very wrong at the same time.

I hear Pablo's phone ring and in a whispered voice, he says, "Oh, hi. Yes. I can't believe I left it there. You know I will be back over there shortly. You too. Oh, and make sure you cover the hickey before you bring the girls."

I pretend I didn't hear the conversation and contemplate my next move. I can't believe my best friend and he are dating behind my back... they will pay!

She walks right in with my girls and I motion her to sit and eat some lasagna. She glances at him for approval and I see he gives her a slight nod.

I hand her a glass of wine and fill his as well. I pour me a glass of Pepsi because the last thing I want to drink is the wine I just put eyedrops from my purse in when retrieving her glass from the cupboard.

The next morning, his parents advise me of their death. Apparent murder-suicide. The notes simply said, "Sorry."

Sorry our relationship ended just like my relationship with my ex-husband... death do you part.

ABOUT THE AUTHOR

CRICKET PEHLEMANN

Hello. I am a new author writing under the pen name of Cricket Pehlemann. I love reading thrillers, mystery, and fantasy, long walks on the beach, and pink ponies. Haha! I currently have two thriller projects in the works and a children's superhero series for my autistic grandson. When I am not working, I try to spend as much time with him as I can. He is amazing, smart, funny, and such a talented artist.

facebook.com/kelly.harwood.9803

instagram.com/KellyHarwood_healthcoach

EDWARD

M. A. SAVINO

THIRD PLACE WINNER

Context: Dating Disasters | **Item:** Glove

Edward sits across from me, a blank expression on his face. This is our third date, but the first time I've spoken about the strange things happening in the house I recently purchased.

"Sounds like a dream," he says, forking chicken into his mouth.

My eyes widen. "This wasn't a dream. I've seen the kid three times now. He runs past me and then disappears."

Edward's hand stops mid-air, his asparagus dropping off his utensil. "What do you mean he *disappears*?"

I shift my chair closer to the table. "I mean, he vanishes into the ceiling!"

An eerie silence settles into the room, and I realize everyone in the restaurant is staring at me.

Edward's hand rests on mine. "Bernice, relax. You're getting worked up over nothing."

"Nothing?" I stand quickly, the back of my knees striking my chair.

I drop my purse on the table, and Edward frowns. "Bernice, what are you doing?"

"Listen, I've enjoyed the last few weeks, but I can't date someone who thinks what I've seen is *nothing*." I drop a one-hundred-dollar bill on the table. "This should cover my meal."

The child's glove I found mocks me from inside my purse. I remove it and toss it onto his unfinished plate. "I found this while I was cleaning."

Edward stares down at it.

I storm away from the table, my heart pounding. The restaurant door bangs open, and arctic air stings my face. A hand grips my bicep tight and spins me around. I scream and instinctively swing, striking Edward in the cheek with a mitten-covered fist. He lets me go at once, and I cover my face with both hands. "I'm so sorry."

He rocks his jaw and raises his brows. "Wow, that's some right hook you have." His eyes light up. "Are you this feisty in the bedroom?"

I glare at him, not in the mood for his humor.

His hands slide around my waist, and his piercing blue eyes lock onto mine. "Show me."

I roll my neck. "Show you what?"

He places his palm on my lower back and directs me to the parking lot. "Let's go to your place, and you can show me where it happened."

"Right now? But I haven't finished unpacking and..."

He places a chilled finger on my lips. "I'm not worried about boxes." He opens the passenger-side door of his car and gestures with a nod. "Come on."

I sink into the passenger seat, and the door slams, startling me. My stomach clenches, and an uneasy feeling floods my body.

"Sorry about the door." He drops into the driver's seat. "The wind caught it."

I gaze through the windshield. The fluffy white flakes float over the top of the car and pile onto the hood. I grip my purse tighter on my lap as he puts the car in drive and fishtails out of the parking lot.

The closer we get to my house, the more the tension inside the car builds. Since bumping into me at the grocery store where we met, he's picked me up twice, but I haven't let him inside—too embarrassed by all the boxes.

I glance at Edward, his eyes fixed on the road.

We pull to the curb, and I exit the car, walking briskly to my front door.

Edward stands on the sidewalk looking at the neighbor's house, holding a black bag in his hand.

"What's in the bag?" I ask as my door pops open.

"A cleansing kit." His eyes flit from the street to mine. "To get rid of your ghost."

"Very funny." I smile half-heartedly.

Edward walks in, and I close the door behind him. My mouth drops open as he strolls away from me, enters the kitchen and stands beneath the spot in the ceiling where the little boy keeps disappearing.

A chill runs down my spine, and the hair on my neck stands.

I never told him *where*.

The floor creaks when I take a step back, and his head whips in my direction. I turn and run, my hand just reaching the door handle, when something strikes me in the back, launching the air from my lungs. I thrash as Edward drags me by my hair from the entryway to the kitchen. I open my mouth to scream, and a fist comes down on my face, breaking my nose with an audible crunch.

Blood drains from my nostrils onto my lips as my body slams into the side of the kitchen island.

I curl into a ball on the floor, unable to move, my heart pounding as he pulls a drill from his bag and removes screws from the shiplap ceiling, taking the wood down piece by piece.

Minutes later, a canvas bag slides from the ceiling, and he sets it on the island.

A small striped glove drops onto my chest, falling off the skeletal remains of a child's hand, hanging over the edge above me. Edward picks up the glove, removes the matching one I gave him from his pocket, and shoves them both in the bag.

My breathing turns shallow, fear coursing through every inch of me. "Why?" I sob.

"He lived next door..." A sinister smile spreads across his face as he points a handgun with a long silencer down at me. "...and he saw something he shouldn't have. Now, so have you."

There's a quick flash and then nothing.

Nothing but silence.

A soft glow appears above me, and the boy extends his ghostly hand.

I take it, and we walk together through my closed front door, following Edward to his car. We sit in his back seat, holding hands as he loads the bags containing our bodies into the trunk, flops behind the wheel and adjusts his mirror, his unseeing eyes peering right through us.

The boy and I are trapped, forced to remain in the space between the living and the dead until someone realizes what he really is.

A monster.

ABOUT THE AUTHOR

M. A. SAVINO

M. A. Savino, aka Melissa Savino, is from the City of Elmira in the Finger Lakes region of New York. She's the mother of four, grandmother to two, and has a Doberman named Pope. Besides her passion for writing, she loves her indoor plant collection and watching crime series with her husband. She finds writing therapeutic and blends real-life experiences and truths about her life into her stories, adding to their authenticity and clearing her mind of repetitive thoughts, dreams, and sometimes painful memories. Now that she has found her passion for storytelling, nothing can stop her.

facebook.com/melissa.savino.33
instagram.com/savinotheauthor
tiktok.com/@savinotheauthor

NEIGHBORHOOD SNAPDRAGONS

ALY STAR

Context: Neighborhood Nightmares | **Item:** Broken Phone

The hairs on the back of my neck prickle and stand as I look out the front window. There he is again, Cedar Blythe, bent over the Snapdragons in the morning light, that smile just a bit too wide, teeth a flash of white, hiding the feral beneath civility. Something deep inside my body tenses when he is near.

I avoid it at any cost, because the thought of being alone with him ties my stomach into knots. It's as if it knows that if he corners me, there will be no escape. I always have my phone handy to fake a call or call for help. Whatever necessary.

Cedar is the life of the party. That doesn't mean I trust him. No one else would understand this fear I have of him. He's the soft-spoken old man at the end of the cul-de-sac in our gated community. He gives children candy with neat little bows and that unwavering smile. He tends the neighborhood garden with that smile locked in place. He is meticulous with the flowers, but laid back with people. Every movement measured.

He checks all the boxes on the Good Guy checklist. But something sinister simmers behind that facade. Some of the ladies in the neighborhood smile just as falsely, but you can still see the strain behind their eyes. In his eyes, there is only a void.

Inhale. Slowly, shaky. One, two, three, four.... Exhale. My lungs burn, my chest tightens; it's like I'm breathing through a straw. I straighten my shoulders and walk to the door, phone clutched in my hand like a lifeline, ready to call for help. The cold doorknob grounds me. If I speed walk to my car, he'll think I'm running late and won't try to make small talk.

I ease the door open, my thumb already on the lock button. The click goes off like a gunshot. I flinch. My heart begins to race. I shut the door quietly behind me and hurry to my Audi.

My name slices through the crisp morning air—calm, sing-song almost, but it spears into my spine. I give a little wave and continue. The handle is cool to the touch. Beeping lets me know my driver's door has unlocked. My palms slicken with sweat as I open the door and slide in, locking it as soon as it closes. The engine hums, and still, I can't shake the feeling of being watched.

As I pull out of my driveway, my eyes flick to the rearview mirror—just to be sure. The day passes in a blur of errands and unease. Even miles away, I can't shake the feeling of eyes on me. At every red light, I check my surroundings. Every time a shop door opens, I glance up to check for Cedar. By the time I head home, my pulse still hasn't settled.

Pulling into my driveway, the neighborhood is deathly silent. No music. No laughter. The whole cul-de-sac feels muted, like the world's been turned down a notch. Even in this rain, there should be activity. No lights in any window or coming from the street lamps. The power must be out. I look around to ensure Cedar isn't lurking. I grab the supplies and ready my keys and phone to make an expeditious entrance through the front door. As I approach, for a heartbeat, I could swear I see a figure in my window—but I blink, and it's gone.

The lock clicks back into place behind me, and I kick my shoes off. Cold from the tile seeps into the soles of my feet.

A creak vibrates through the house. I freeze, holding my breath, trying to identify where it came from. Laying my packages and keys on the table in the entryway, I toggle the flashlight on my phone. Slowly, I walk into the kitchen.

A tarp lies in the middle of the floor, where my dining table used to be. Shivers crawl up my spine and ripple through my body. Arms, strong and sudden, wrap around me, crushing my ribs. Twisting, I put my entire strength into getting out of the hold, but to no avail. I attempt to unlock my phone, intending to call for help. Before I'm able, it is violently knocked from my hands.

Pain radiates from the base of my skull as I'm hit in the back of the head. I kick back and land a solid hit to my attacker's leg. I'm thrown forward, my body cracking as I hit the wall and fall. Blackness encroaches on my vision as I reach for my phone. Relief floods my veins as I grab the slick metal. I click to unlock it, but the crack spiderwebbing my screen dashes that relief immediately.

Laughter cuts through the silence. I look up to see Cedar standing above me, humor in his eyes. The shadows illuminate the darkness in his smile. For the first time since I met him, his smile seems genuine. His eyes are alight with amusement.

"You can keep the broken thing. It will do you no good," he says in the same voice he uses to praise block party hostesses. A ringing fills my ears, and the last thing I see is the bottom of his usual Hey Dudes before everything fades away.

Some time later, I watch the neighborhood garden through spectral eyes. There he was again, Cedar Blythe, bent over the Snapdragons, that smile just a bit too wide, teeth a flash of white, mask hiding the darkness within firmly. The bucket he uses for fertilizer now holds composted remains of the latest victim: me. Flesh degraded for the Snapdragons, bones ground to powder, mixed thoroughly, waiting to bring life from my death.

A boy runs close by. Cedar's smile stretches impossibly wider as he says, "Remember, if you play in the soil, wash your hands immediately when you're done. You don't want to get sick." His eyes glance from the boy to my empty house across the street, sentinel as if holding its breath, waiting for my return.

ABOUT THE AUTHOR

ALY STAR

A lifelong book lover turned new author, Aly Star has been an avid reader since childhood. Southern-born and spitefully fueled, she blesses hearts and stands firm in what she believes—especially when it comes to her kid. A proud single mom, she wrangles a household featuring her kid, two dogs (all with "P" names—an accident, allegedly), and one cat—the only girl, the only rebel, and the undisputed overlord of the pandemonium.

When she's not busy "momming" or binging horror movies with her bestie, she's usually buried in a book from one of many genres she loves. Whether it's a chilling thriller or a nail-biting romance, she believes every story holds a little magic between its pages. Writing and sharing her own stories brings a spark of joy to her wonderfully neuro-atypical world.

facebook.com/alystarpa
instagram.com/book_dragon_aly
tiktok.com/@alystar04

CREEP HOUSE

STEPHANIE TELLAS

Context: Spooky Season | **Item:** Candle

Angie and her sister LJ were taking a jog on a dark cloudy gloomy day. LJ spotted a vacant black house with an unlocked black picket fence. The house was a little cracked open; she wanted to go in and take a peek. “Angie lets go see what is inside” begged LJ. “No, it looks to creepy” replied Angie. “If you’re not going to go with me, then I will go alone”. LJ proceeds to open the little gate of the picket fence and ascended the stairs. “Wait for me!” Shouted Angie. She ran through the gate and met her sister up by the door. LJ knocked but received no answer.

In the living room there was an old tan recliner, white

couch with flower design on them and there was a winding staircase. Couples with creepy faces held their poses in photographs as if they were watching the sisters.

Both sisters heard music screeching to life, like a record starting. They looked at each other. "Sounds like it coming from upstairs, said LJ. I hundred percent don't feel comfortable going upstairs, this house gives me the creeps". "Suit yourself. You can stay downstairs if you want. I'm going to go explore and see where it is coming from. LJ tiptoed upstairs while leaving her anxious sister behind.

Angie waited for a couple of minutes.

"LJ! Where are you? I am coming upstairs!"

Her footsteps creeped up the stairs. Once at the top, she saw that there were two bedrooms. one with a nursery, a crib, a changing table, laden with diapers, wipes, and toys.

Another bedroom with theme décor of nightmare before Christmas. There was also a bathroom upstairs that just looked creepy. The same eerie photographs of couples that were downstairs were positioned upstairs as well. The bathtub was filled with red water; this was making Angie more uncomfortable being by herself and not sure exactly where her sister had gone when she went upstairs. Angie looked around each room but found no trace of LJ.

"LJ are you downstairs? Hello!" Angie scurried back downstairs to see if her sister was there somewhere. Angie scours around the living room, but no sign of LJ.

Angie went to the kitchen where the cabinets were black. The kitchen had black countertops, a black fridge, and a black stove. The kitchen also had a black island to bring the black décor together. She still couldn't find her sister. "Hello, where are you?"

No answer, Angie headed back upstairs.

Angie swore she heard her sister. "Angie! Can you hear me!!!".

"LJ where are you?"

Sounds rattle off near the staircase. Angie ran downstairs thinking her sister had somehow ended up there.

Angie looked at the photos by the staircase and screamed. "It's LJ face she saw in the picture mouthing, "Help me!" Angies heart thudded. Do I call 911?

LJ repeats again "Help!"

Angie is transfixed at the picture her sister is stuck in. and said to LJ "We'll figure a way to get you out.

"Please hurry! LJ said from the picture. "I only have a certain amount of time before I become one of them". "Help me fast !!"

Angie sprinted out of the house and saw some kids walking by.

"Please help me my sister is stuck in this creepy house." The kids followed Angie to the house, one of them, upon seeing LJ in the frame said, "I watch these movies about how get ghosts out of these pictures. We can try it."

"What would that be?" asked Angie. "We can take a shop vac."

"That's not going to work, that's just like only in the movies, like Ghostbusters". Another kid pipped up. Then maybe we can try like a séance, where they put candles around like they are going to have the souls come out of their body". "Maybe I can put candles near the photos." "Maybe we can get a pastor as well."

"Help!! Please hurry I'm running out of time". Angie wailed LJ.

"We will go get a pastor fast".

The kids and Angie ran to a church not too far from the creepy house and finding pastor engaged in prayer. "Pastor please help us my sister is stuck in this photo with these people who have creepy faces, if we don't get her out fast, she'll become one of them. Please help us, begged Angie". "Let's go, I will see what I can do", said the pastor.

The pastor, Angie, and the kids returned to the house, running up to the middle of the staircase. The pastor sets up the candles, lit them, and begin praying what sounded like Latin. The prayer however ineffectual. "You're all running out of time; I have until midnight. I have five minutes before I become one of them".

The clock was ticking fast; Angie and LJ were screaming "Pastor figure something out and fast! "I don't know what else to try." The clock struck midnight; Angie and LJ are trying to reach each other's hands. The other people with creepy faces pulled Angie right into the picture with LJ. The Pastor and the kids screamed and ran away from the house. Nobody heard from Angie and LJ again.

ABOUT THE AUTHOR

STEPHANIE TELLAS

Married to high school sweetheart for almost 24 yrs been together longer. We have 2 special needs kids, and we take care of our 11 month old special needs niece. We have 2 lovely fur kids, sunny 4 1/2yrs old poodle mix, and rascal 10yr old black and white domestic cat. I was born in KS, husband and kids were born in Az. I have been in Az since I was little. I love to read, do adult coloring, and crossword puzzles. I also network animals.

Join my Facebook group: Psychological Thriller Authors and Readers Unite

VANISHED

TINA S TRANSFORMATION

FINALIST

Context: Neighborhood Nightmares | **Item:** Note

The letter was waiting in the mailbox before dawn.

There was no stamp and no postmark. My name was scrawled across the front in my own handwriting.

For a moment, I just stared at it. *What the hell is this? I don't remember writing this.*

I unfolded the page.

At 7:42 tonight, a child's scream will shatter the cul-de-sac. A life will end.

I read it twice, my skin prickling. *This has to be some kind of sick prank.* I crumpled the note and tossed it on the counter, refusing to give it more thought.

But at exactly 7:42 that evening, a scream tore through the street. The sound was so sharp it jolted me to my feet. Neighbors rushed outside, voices rising in panic. A little girl from three houses down had been struck by a car backing out of a driveway. She died instantly.

The next afternoon, another letter waited for me. This time, I didn't open it right away. My hands shook. When I finally tore the flap, the words punched the air from my lungs.

By the time the moon rises, death will walk through your home. The next life to end will be someone you love. You will see their last moments, and there is nothing you can do. Every door you open, every shadow you chase—one will be your own. Pray you recognize it before it's too late.

Soon, every house had a letter. Everyone admitted the handwriting matched their own. People clutched the notes as if they were cursed relics. Some neighbors barricaded their doors, while others sat on porches in silence, watching the hours crawl by until their fates arrived.

By the third day, I couldn't sleep. I sat at the window, staring at the row of mailboxes standing like sentries. It can't be real. This isn't possible. There has to be an explanation.

That was when I saw him.

In the thin gray light before dawn, a figure moved between the boxes. He walked slowly, slipping envelopes into each one.

It was Mr. Harris. He lived in the corner house, at least that is what everyone said. But as I watched him, a cold knot twisted in my gut. When had he moved in? Why could I not remember? His blinds were always drawn closed. His yard was perfect, frozen and still, like a scene trapped behind glass. Sometimes, I thought I saw him standing in the shadows, but when I blinked, he was gone. The house did not feel lived in. It felt staged.

I couldn't stop myself. I grabbed my jacket and stepped outside. The grass was wet beneath my shoes.

"Mr. Harris," I called, my voice breaking.

He turned. The streetlight caught his face, and the sight froze me. Why does he look familiar? Where do I know him from? His features seemed blurred, like my own reflection in rippling water.

"You shouldn't be awake," he said, his voice calm, almost gentle. He slid one last envelope into my mailbox. "This one is for you."

My pulse hammered as I pulled it free. My name stretched across the front in the same neat strokes I had used my entire life. No. No, this can't be mine. I didn't write this. I couldn't have.

I opened it with shaking hands.

Tonight, you will vanish. No one will remember you lived here. No one will speak your name again.

My head swam. Vanish? What does that mean? Is this some kind of threat? Am I losing my mind?

I looked up to confront him, but the street was empty. He was gone.

My heart pounded as I ran toward the corner house. The windows were black voids, the porch was bare. I hammered on the door until my fists ached. No sound came from inside. No movement at all.

When I turned back, the cul-de-sac was the same, yet everything felt distant. I could see the houses, the neat lawns, the quiet street, but I was not part of it anymore. I could watch, I could notice the small details, the swing swaying in a yard, a curtain twitching, but I could not step forward, could not touch anything. It was my neighborhood, and yet it was not. I was there, and I was gone.

The mailboxes were closed, every one of them. Porch lights flicked on, and neighbors stepped out, squinting at me as though I were a trespasser.

"Who are you?" one of them asked.

It was Linda. Just last week, she had borrowed sugar from me. My voice cracked. "It's me. From number nine."

"There is no number nine," Linda said. Her face was blank, her tone certain. She pointed at the end of the street.

I followed her gaze. Where my house had stood was only an empty lot, flat and bare. No porch. No front door. No sign that anyone had ever lived there.

The breath left my body. This isn't real. I'm here. I live here. Don't I?

The letter in my hands faded as I stared at it. The ink dissolved, the note paling until it was nothing but a blank sheet.

And then I was gone.

The cul-de-sac fell silent. The neighbors returned to their homes. By morning, no one remembered a family had ever lived at the end of the street. That was how the first of the Neighborhood Nightmares began.

ABOUT THE AUTHOR

TINA S TRANSFORMATION

Meet the AUTHOR of your nightmares

Like the Freddy Krueger of authors, Tina S Transformation doesn't just write nightmares—she traps you in them.

Not the kind you shake off in the AM. The kind that lingers. The kind that clings when you close your eyes at night and whispers when you're alone. The kind that drags you back again and again until you can't escape.

Every twisted word pulls you deeper. Every page leaves you gasping. Every story reminds you why you both love and fear the dark.

So, step inside. Where shadows breathe and monsters never sleep. What goes past blood and bone, what creeps under your skin until you're scratching at the edges of reality and begging for escape.

Once you start reading... there's no way out. Check in now... if you dare.

facebook.com/tinastransformationauthor

instagram.com/authortinastransformation

tiktok.com/@tinastransformation338

ECHOES OF HER SCREAMS

MIRA VISE

Context: Dating Disasters | **Item:** Shoe

Puddles splashed as her sneakers hit the pavement. Beads of sweat danced across her face. Her hair was matted and snarled. Yellow and purple bruises cover her body. Red, swollen marks circled her wrists and ankles. Cuts - fresh, scabbed, and scarred - riddle her skin. She gasped, desperately pulling air into her lungs. Her clothes were heavy and cold from the rain. Thunder booms. Lightning flashes. Smoke billowed behind her. No matter how much her body screamed and hurt, she couldn't stop. She was free.

Two years of doctors, nurses, therapists, medications, and hospital stays. Time should heal all wounds. In her case, it didn't. Sometimes the damage is too deep. And there is no coming back, it creates this hidden being, a monster.

A new message pinged an alert on Abigail's phone. She quickly entered her passcode. Without hesitation, she typed out a reply:

I'd love to get drinks with you on Friday.

Her phone pinged back:

I can't wait.

Images entered her mind, and a sinister smirk appeared on her lips. She stared at Jacob's photo. "You are right. We are going to have fun," she murmured, sliding her finger over him, "just not the kind you are hoping for."

Friday finally arrived. Abigail laid out a pink, knee-length dress, sparkly flats, and her lucky necklace. "*Monster*" by Skillet blared on repeat, setting in motion her date night routine: a bubble bath, make-up, hair, and a glass of her favorite wine.

The parking lot was half empty when Abigail pulled in. Parking her car, she looked in the mirror, took a deep breath, and headed inside. The bar was nicer than she expected, though a hint of stale beer and greasy food filled the air. She scanned the room and saw Jacob waving her over. He didn't move from his seat when she approached, just gestured toward the empty chair. She sat, already annoyed.

After a couple of rounds, Jacob hinted about heading to the diner next door. "I've got a better idea," Abigail suggested, her eyes playful. "We could go back to my place, order pizza and watch a movie?"

In quick agreement, they left.

Abigail could hardly contain her excitement as they walked into her house. She leads him to the living room. "Make yourself comfortable. I'll go grab us some drinks."

Jacob yawned right on cue. She watched his eyes become heavy as she looked his way. The movie continued…but all she could hear were her caged demons ready to play.

His eyelids finally fell, and his breath began to slow. She gently shook him. When he didn't stir, she began.

The floorboards squeaked overhead. The door whined as she opened it. A dank smell welcomed her. Her bare feet smacking the cement grew louder as she neared. She sat amongst the shadows, seething with anger, watching and waiting. A small smirk appeared when Jacob's eyes fluttered open. He looked confused. His naked body quivered from the icy, cold air. She flipped a switch that turned on a dim bulb. The light was just enough to envelop his tense body. He panicked, tugging at his restraints, eyes scanning the darkness beyond.

The yellow glow cast upon her half-naked, scarred body as she emerged. Jacob's face whitened. Beads of sweat lined his forehead. His confusion turned to pure fear. Like a cat teasing its prey, Abigail circled, gently touching him. Not saying a word. She could feel him trembling. His mouth opened as he tried to speak. She caressed his face. Her eyes penetrated deep into his, making him really see her- the darkness he had helped to create.

"You look a bit surprised. Maybe you weren't expecting to see me again?" Abigail walked into the shadows. Returning, she holds up a wig and latex skin. His eyes widened. "I thought for sure my voice would give me away," she raged with sudden anger, "Oh, that's right, you only heard my screams and whimpers of pain." Throwing the wig and latex aside, she taps his nose, "Now it's my turn."

Slowly, she reached down, curling her fingers around the wooden handle. Swiftly, she brandished a stained knife before his eyes. He tried to move. Leather belts kept him rigidly in place. Placing the blade to his cheek, ruby liquid dribbled down the steel.

Tilting her head, she admired the sticky residue. Her mouth salivated. She puts the blade to her lips, licking. Tasting.

Lunging forward, the sharp edge glided through. The cuts were precise and meticulously planned. She yells with each slash:

"You held me down!"

"You violated me!"

"You laughed!"

"Scars!"

"Memories!"

"Nightmares!"

"It wasn't a GAME!!"

Jacob's screams shot through the night. He wailed in pain as she sliced his skin. He begged her to stop.

Her eyes blackened. The world went blank. The demons inside took over. She growled, grunted, and shrieked. Swinging and stabbing. His vital fluids flew, spraying and splattering, coating the room.

All at once, it was deathly quiet, nothingness.

Abigail's face and body were painted in crimson red. The smell of iron and sweat lingered in the space. His brutally battered body slouched, only the ropes and buckles holding him up. Her body shook. Her heart pounded inside her chest, adrenaline coursing through her veins. She paced the floor, eyes trained on him, soaking in this moment. Her blissful revenge.

Snapping her fingers, "Monster" by Skillet began to play.

Bloody footsteps and drippings trail her as she makes her way to the murder map. Stepping in front of Jacob's picture, she raised her arm and with her blood-soaked hand, placed an X. Abigail stepped back, admiring her work. She silently whispered, "Four down".

Her phone pinged, a new message appeared. Her deadly stare focused on Mark. A devilish grin spread across her face as she replied:

I would love to get some drinks with you.

ABOUT THE AUTHOR

MIRA VISE

Mira Vise is a debut author who knows a thing or two about fighting back-not just against monsters on a page, but in real life as a survivor of stage 4a colon cancer. She is an avid reader of all things terrifying, with a passion for thrillers and horror. Drawing inspiration from the indie authors she admires, she penned Echoes of Her Screams. Mira loves spooky and finds comfort in the dark. She lives in the mitten state with her husband, four children, and her animals, and can be found beneath the vast, starry sky, hoping to catch a glimpse of the Northern lights.

instagram.com/iluvfrogs

ACKNOWLEDGMENTS

A huge thank you to all the authors who shared their time, creativity, and words for this contest, and followed through to publication. You should be incredibly proud of what you've accomplished.

To our readers: your enthusiasm, feedback, and support made this contest truly exhilarating. You're not just reading these tales—you're helping many of these authors take their first steps into the world of writing. Your feedback helps us grow, and your support and encouragement makes this journey truly special.

Thank you to everyone who shared this contest, invited others to join and read, and to all the Facebook groups who welcomed our promotion. The support in this community means everything.

And finally, thank you to our finalist judges:

- **Ashley Coffey:** admin of Psychological Thriller Readers Facebook group
- **Rachel Graham:** author of *Follow Me* and admin of KILLER THRILLERS Facebook group

- **Mark Jenkins:** author of *Do Unto Others* and *So Shall You Reap*, and admin of PSYCHOLOGICAL THRILLERS BOOK CLUB Facebook group
- **Daniel McBreakneck:** blogger at Avid Readers Club - Share the Love
- **William Nuessle:** novelist, screenwriter and proud member of Supporting Beginner Writers Facebook group
- **Brian O'Sullivan:** author of *The Bartender* and *The Photo Album*
- **Keeley Webb:** author of *Whispers in the Wine Cellar* and *Killer Content*

This contest and publication is part of the *Author: Unlocked* initiative, dedicated to helping aspiring authors take the leap into writing and self-publishing. Your support has launched these authors into the world. We can't wait to see where they go next.

Learn more at:

author-unlocked.rachgrahamreads.com

www.ingramcontent.com/pod-product-compliance
Lightning Source LLC
Chambersburg PA
CBHW020459310726
48979CB00016B/2723/J

* 9 7 8 1 0 6 7 0 1 1 5 9 8 *